Circling the Inferno

Short Stories

Joan Drescher Cooper

ISBN 978-1-62806-364-6 (print | paperback)

Library of Congress Control Number 2023914566

Published by Salt Water Media
29 Broad Street, Suite 104
Berlin, MD 21811
www.saltwatermedia.com

Cover art by unsplash.com user Alexey Demidov
Cover and interior design by Salt Water Media

Author website: www.joandcooper.com

Circling the Inferno

Acknowledgements

Thank you to my mother, daughter, and husband for listening to these stories as they evolved. The writers of the Salisbury Writers Group (Rabbit Gnaw Writers live on!) helped me to clean up the convoluted sentences and get on with the story-telling.

Previous publishers of these works include:

"Blessing the Bakery of the Saints" *River Babble*, 2015

"Celia's Audience with a Madman," *The Bay to Ocean Anthology*, 2020.

"Circling the Inferno" *Write Launch Magazine*, January 2022.

Contents

Persephone Leaves

This April morning, ice spiderwebs raced across the surface of the ditch filled with yesterday's rain. The dog sniffed it suspiciously and hesitated with a paw raised. Skittering robins distracted her, so she urged us on. The breeze nipped with chill. "Persephone's gone back for one more kiss," you said under your breath.

You meant to be funny, but I fail to see the humor. Women never fail to fall for the villain, the rogue, the troubled one. Goddesses are no different.

I imagine him waiting for her. He'd be broody with dark fire in his eyes. She likes his darkness. She enjoys the contrast between his cold and her warmth. She makes excuses for his vile behavior and begs to return to him.

What's a parent to do, after all? She cries for her lover all night, you let her go, and then the frost returns, nips the fingers, tightens the buds. Ice crystals dust everything the day she leaves the surface. Our breath blows white as we walk that morning. You say, "No worries, old man. She will return."

When she arrives at the gate, Erebus balks at Persephone's request—a moment with her husband. "Sweetie. Peri, darling. He's busy poling people across the Styx."

"I am the Goddess of the Spring. You cannot deny a goddess," she tries to puff herself up with confidence, but the shyness of the unopened flower gives her away. "Please?"

Erebus eyes the wand of green wheat braided into a whip that she twists in her hands. "You just left. Give 'em a break."

"Come on, Ere. I just want to see him one more time before I'm banished for three months." She sighs it out just like Gloria Swanson in *Sunset Boulevard*, which she just watched on TCM during a late-night chat with her mom.

Erebus speaks into his wrist and frowns then he steps out of her path. The underworld erupts in geysers of fire, smoke with a tinge of brimstone, and the sound of wails. Persephone glances down at the pathway and sees cigarette butts scattered in the sparse grass, trash clogs the gutters. Erebus says, "He makes a mess when you're gone."

"Then I'll do a bit of a spring cleaning while I visit." Persephone giggles and steps toward the path to their place.

Erebus shrugs. "Ah well. On to twiddle with the damned," he says as he walks away.

Gliding down the pathway, Persephone muses, "I've done not too much harm." She counts on her fingers. "I've started all the cold-weather crops, touched the crocus, seen to the hyacinth, and surely the daffodils can laugh their full heads off without me." She traipses down the long fiery hallway to their golden chambers, avoiding eye contact with the spirits watching from the walls. She concludes, "Perhaps mother allowed this visit for solace. It's a big responsibility being the god of the underworld."

She winces when she finally shuts the door on their apartment and stares at the dishes stacked up in the sink. The air smells of mold and stale cigarette smoke though he said he's given it up along with the whiskey. Empty bottles are evident under the sink. She cleans all day and recycles everything she can. She thinks of all the winter buds—those plastic-colored hyacinths blooming without her. The forsythia will burst into yellow despite the cold.

Hades comes home to a clean apartment and his little goddess all aglow on the sofa watching a murder mystery. He says, "Erebus tried to reach me earlier—sorry, it's this blasted virus." He is tired and red-eyed. Smoke rises from his shoulders.

Persephone shrugs. "I forgot what I wanted. You know what? It was a pigsty in here."

He shrugs, and a thousand souls shriek. She never noticed that before. She rises from the couch and gives him a quick kiss. "I thought I wanted you, but I guess I was wrong. See you in September, H."

He catches her close. His breath is all sulfur. She sighs because she loves him—even the acrid breath and bad manners. "Remember I love you, Peri." His mouth descends and holds her captive.

In the morning, the ice was gone from the ditches, and the fragile, waxy dogwoods bloomed in every front yard, every thicket, or forgotten roadside. We walked with the old dog and talked about our children—hers and mine. The crocus burst forth, purple and yellow, through the skim of snow. "Do you think she'll be happy?" Demeter asked as she clutched at my arm.

I laughed, and the world burst into diamonds of yellow sunlight. The temperatures climbed above temperate and warmed the whole world. It is good to be Zeus in the spring. It is good to be kind to the demigods and their sweet human playthings.

Go and Catch a Falling Star

After unpacking the overfilled coolers into the fridge, Sally carried her bags into the borrowed bedroom and took a steadying breath. She closed her eyes and tried to shut out the noise of the rest of the family making plans for lunch on the boardwalk. Like lemmings, they returned to the same beach cottage on the second week of June every year. She rolled her shoulders to release the knots from driving and toting everything into the house.

Sinking down on the bed, she opened her eyes and scanned the bookshelf a few inches from her knees. Between a thick tome of Shakespeare's plays and a few gardening books, the green spine of the collected works of John Donne gleamed with old gold lettering. She smiled at it like you greet an old friend. She was beginning to reach for it when Charlie banged into the room, his big suitcase bumping into the door and the dresser.

His words were garbled. "Why'd ya haf ta chuse dis room, agin, Sal?" He hoisted the case onto the bed, jostling her. "Aren't we payin' for the lot?" Working his words around a mouthful of something snatched from the fridge, he sounded rude. He had refused to stop on the road for a meal. Sally stared at her husband and thought about all the idiosyncrasies she had not bothered to tally before they married last year. Had he always been this gruff? This cheap?

Sally tried to smile, but her mouth hurt after pretending to grin at the rest of the family as her stomach grumbled for the last hour. "I know, Charlie. But I like this room. I always stay in here."

The room was small, tucked in a corner of the first floor under the stairs of the two-floor cottage. Probably meant for a study or a child's room, someone jammed a full-size bed inside to increase the occupancy in the rental brochure. Sally liked the room long before the full-size bed. Long before she discovered Donne and his secrets—she had spent childhood years monitoring the movements of everyone by their measured tread on the stairs. Sally watched people—her favorite occupation. She could fill diaries with observations about other people.

"I'll unpack for you, Charlie," she said.

"Thanks, sweetie." He winked at her. When had he started to wink? "I'll see if I can make us a couple of sandwiches to tide us over till dinner."

Nodding at him, Sally said nothing. Was he worried about money? They never talked about money. How could she start that conversation?

Her mother and father had never discussed finances in front of her. They never needed to make grand pronouncements because all she needed to do was keep an eye on the dwindling weight of paper bag lunches and smaller portions at dinner. When she was ten, her older sister ran off to get married, her brother signed up with the Army, and her father received a promotion. Family reunions at the beach started because her brother was back on leave that next June. In the following years, whether the rest of the family could make it or not, her parents scrimped and saved for the little beach house way back in the pines. Last year her parents retired and talked about staying home, so Sally took a turn, contacted the realtor, and paid for the week.

After she layered one of the drawers with Charlie's cotton shirts, Sally couldn't resist pulling the thin book from between its neighbors and opening to the back. She stared down at the alternating writing—hers so loopy and feminine and the other, a bold, darker script. Snatches of lines of poetry to start, a question, and an answer. Another partial line from the metaphysical poet, then a returning jibe of interpretation. She had been trading messages with this other reader for fifteen years.

Finding the book had been happenstance, but she'd kept the relationship going since. This room changed over the years, but the bookshelf had remained stocked with the same classics. The gardening books opened to fine pen and ink illustrations that someone had daubed with watercolors, but the collection of old poetry might have remained untouched. Ten years old, she had slid it out on a whim, opened at random, and found "Go and catch a falling star/Get with child a mandrake root" which made her blush. What was a mandrake root? And who was going to capture a star—that trailing light in the night sky she'd once spied on the beach?

Listening for Charlie, Sally opened to the spot automatically and let her eyes rake the poem—every word—without seeking sense or meaning. When she was ten, she had written the lines on an envelope and tucked them in the back. That's where she found the writing the next year. That's where she'd begun her part of the two hands of conversation exploding across the back pages left blank by the publisher. That happy blankness was now filled with ideas—opinions—lines quoted and extrapolated in tandem.

She remembered burning with the desire to take the book with her. To take it home like a talisman. Instead, she left it there after agonizing what to write for the rest of the week. She looked for the book first thing every time she visited—her lucky charm in the tiny bedroom of the beach cottage.

She did not know who her correspondent might be. Once when the owners stopped in to say hello, she eyed the two elderly sisters and wondered if they knew about John Donne and the messages. Young or old, man or woman—it hardly mattered though she had dreamed of a boy with dark hair and eyes like Donne.

She heard Charlie calling her name and jumped. She slid the thin volume back into place and left the room with the dresser drawers still open as if she had been caught in some covert act.

After a walk and an ice cream cone they shared, Sally and Charlie found the house empty. He began a tour-like inventory of the bedrooms, the kitchen, and porch. "I want to lie down for a bit," Sally said, excusing herself.

She fell asleep with Donne's collected poems clutched to her chest. When she woke, Charlie lay beside her, his hand beside her shoulder, large and warm like she had become accustomed. The house was still quiet though someone had turned on the radio in the kitchen. As she strained to hear the tune, she fell asleep and dreamed she danced with John Donne. Starstruck, she couldn't think of one thing to say to amuse him. He kept time by tapping on her shoulder.

She opened her eyes to Charlie rubbing her back and saying, "Hey, Sal. Time to wake up. Dinner's in five." He gave her half a crooked grin and looked away.

"What's wrong?" she asked.

"We'll talk later," he said, stood up, and joined the others in the kitchen.

Sally felt woozy with sleep during the meal. She noticed Charlie watching her from across the table. He ate and excused himself before dessert. When she looked for him on the front porch, he was gone.

Returning to their room, Sally straightened the bed and smiled, thinking about dancing with John Donne. Rather silly. Donne had married his one true love and written all that poetry for her. She ran a hand over the bed and under the pillow. She crouched down and looked on the floor for the small, leather-bound book. Sally ran a finger over the spines of the books on the shelf where she usually found it. Unsettled, she returned to the porch to keep an eye out for Charlie.

He arrived with a tote of caramel popcorn and a box of peanut butter fudge. "Your mom said she loves it, but the line was too long today." He lifted the bags in a shrug, "I'll be right back."

Sally nodded. She stared out at the street in the dimming light, her mind still consumed by the missing book. He returned with a glass of water and handed it to her. "You need to stay hydrated, Sal. You really passed out this afternoon."

She took a sip, noting the lemon wedge she preferred. As he sat next to her on the porch swing, she glanced over at him. What was going on?

He sighed and leaned back. "Sally?"

"Yes?" She took another little sip. A tingle of foreboding raced through her.

"We've been married about a year . . ."

"We're celebrating next month. You know that," she scolded.

"We didn't make any big rules between us."

"True." Sally put the glass down on the side table and angled toward him. He was looking straight out into the street.

"Well, maybe we need a few."

"Like?"

"No secrets."

Sally let go of a little scoffing laugh. She said, "I thought that came with the ceremony." She thought about the cost of the beach house that she had paid with a few bonuses. She considered his thrifty refusal to squander money on lunch. She nodded. "Yes. It's time we talked about things. I was just thinking about that today."

His shoulders relaxed a bit. He brought his left hand up to his lap. He cradled a small rectangular package. "I got you this at that nice bookstore you were talking about. I thought we could both make entries in it."

Sally blushed. Was he talking debits and credits? She kept a bill book at home where she tracked their expenses and savings. Hadn't they ever discussed money? She clumsily took the package as he offered it.

Sliding the contents out into her lap, Sally was confused. Instead of a household ledger, he had given her a small hardback which bore the portrait of a man in ringlets wearing a tall black hat. She turned it over in her hand and finally read "John Donne—Collected Meditations and Poems" written in fancy black script. She opened to the title page and saw his scrawl. "For Sally—Let's keep our secrets together. I love you, Charlie."

Sally felt her cheeks burn with embarrassment. "I guess I should have told you about it. But, Charlie, this is so sweet. This is better than any anniversary present." Her heart was racing when she looked back at him and saw he held the small, green book.

"I hafta say, I was jealous when I recognized your handwriting." He opened it up to the back and looked down in the poor light. "Then I read it through while you were sleeping. It's like a diary—you started those back and forth messages a long time ago."

She nodded. "Since before I understood much more than 'go and catch a falling star.' I still like that one the best."

"I gotta tell you, Sal. I like some of those meditations, but the poetry leaves me numb."

Sally let a nervous laugh erupt. She said, "They are a little dense. I had to look them up at the library most of the time."

"Any idea who is writing back to you?" He leaned back and

set the swing rocking gently. He extended an arm across the backrest, and she took it as a signal to slide over toward him.

"None. Maybe I should leave my name in there this year."

"Maybe. Maybe not. Mysteries are fun, but let's not have secrets, sweetie."

They rocked for a few minutes. Sally looked up at Charlie and said, "While we're talking about ground rules, let's talk about finances."

Beach House Blues

For years, our family rented a Rehoboth Beach house during the third week in June to start our summer vacation. Every winter, my father and I took a daytrip to the beach to choose the vacation rental from the realtor's antique Rolodex and then drive through the sleepy Delaware town to scope them out. We always picked a different place.

The promise of that week in June spurred us through the doldrums of late winter. My sons found the houses creepy—with strange noises at night, but once we adjusted to the place, we enjoyed our week—rain or shine. None of the houses were truly remarkable until we stayed at the house on Brooklyn Avenue.

Brooklyn was one of the few houses left to rent the year we put off our daytrip until late March. It was not beachy—it was mustard yellow and brown with weird bumped-out additions. But it was cheap, had generous off-street parking, and just enough room for the ten of us. The owner, a barrel-chested, grizzly-faced man, was living in the place and gave us a quick tour of his bachelor messiness. He gestured to a decrepit piano crowding the porch, saying, "Don't worry—I'm getting rid of that heap before you come." We shrugged off the presence of the piano and rented Brooklyn on the spot.

When we arrived that June, the house was suspiciously clear of clutter, and the carpet was new. We hauled our bags up the creaky stairs and housed all the kids in the largest bedroom. That left my parents on the first-floor in a tiny bedroom next to the kitchen. They both rose early, so it was perfect. My father set up camp on the front porch like he always did. One or two grandchildren were always with him. The piano was gone.

The whole time, I kept hearing a song—you know how one gets stuck in your head? This song was bouncy and way too loud as my sister and her family arrived well after dark from New England.

I wasn't the only one bothered by music. My oldest son moved out onto the porch to sleep on the second night because "the other kids are keeping me up with their crazy singing." He was a good three years older than the rest, so we approved.

We frequented our usual vacation haunts and walked the boardwalk with the kids. The whole time, even at the noisy arcade, I had that bluesy, boogie-woogie tune stuck in my head.

On Wednesday morning, I woke up to one of those dreams where someone is shouting your name, but this time, it was the crash of piano chords for the chorus of that blues song. After I opened my eyes to the unfamiliar ceiling, I swear the song continued at full volume. Needing coffee, I threw on shorts and a top.

While the old pot percolated, I cut up potatoes and onions for hashed browns and tried to hum the tune. I'm sure it was slightly off-key—but I was still trying to name it. I laid out a pound of bacon on a scratched griddle. I hummed a little louder and almost remembered the words. "I'm as blue as I can be?" I sang under my breath.

My son came into the kitchen from his nest of blankets on the porch swing and sat beside me on a stool. I took a glass out of the cupboard and retrieved chocolate milk from the fridge for him. He usually blurted out everything he was thinking, but he was quiet that morning, sitting there with his hair flattened by sleep. I started to hum again. I uncapped the milk and started to pour.

He asked, "Mom? Do you hear that song playing in your head all the time?"

"What?' I asked. The milk sloshed over the rim.

"That song you're humming? I can hear it. Sometimes it's just piano. Sometimes there's singing."

I grasped at an explanation. "Maybe we heard it on the way down here."

He shook his head. "No. Granddad can hear it, too." He rolled his eyes because my father had probably used his question about the song to launch into a lecture. His lectures were epic and endless.

I picked up the glass to wipe the bottom. I was about to ask the title, when he began to sing in a high, pitchy voice:

Got dem Saint Louis blues I'm as blue as ah can be
Like a man done throwed that rock down into de sea . . .

I almost dropped the glass. My first reaction was to make an excuse like I always did when my son said something uncanny. I plunked down the glass and sloshed more milk onto the counter. I said, "We must have heard it playing on the boardwalk."

Shaking his head, my son sat there, studying me, sipping his milk, and drawing circles on the counter from the spill.

Behind me on the stove, the bacon started to burn. I turned away to salvage the charred parts. I asked, "When did you learn that song?" This was the kid who almost failed fifth grade but scored genius numbers on IQ tests. I never knew what would come out of his mouth.

"It kept playing last night. Over and over."

My father walked into the kitchen carrying a newspaper. "Hey," he said. "Did you know the bacon's burning?"

My son said, "I like it like that." Then he laughed as I transferred the bacon onto a paper towel, and some of the strips crumbled into cinders.

Dad poured another cup of coffee for both of us and dumped milk into them. He said, "Hey. Leave that for a minute and come out onto the porch."

I thought he was hinting that I wasn't relaxing into vacation mode. He patted the makeshift bed my son had made of the swing. He sat next to me. After a few minutes, he said, "I don't hear it now." He sighed. "That song is too much."

"What?"

"Look. I know you're trying to expose the kids to all kinds of art and music...but can you lay off the Bessie Smith revival until your mom and I leave on Friday?"

"Dad! What are you talking about?"

"Look. I haven't slept well this week. Every time I wake up, your kid is playing the 'Saint Louis Blues' at top volume."

"He isn't, Dad." Through the open door beside us, I listened to my son talking to my sister as she poured coffee. Her voice was shrill as my mother came out of the little bedroom. "Who was playing the piano all night?"

My mother, a true German who did not believe in anything but the rational, said, "I know. It's that old Bessie Smith song my uncle liked so much."

I looked over at my father to see if he'd heard. He was frowning. Then my sister's husband, who was nothing if not dense, burst into the room complaining, "What the hell were you all playing this morning?"

My son giggled and began to sing again, but this time, he sounded even more like Bessie Smith. My sister's husband joined the singing. Dad and I looked at each other.

Please understand that we've stayed in vacation places with bats, snakes, and big insects; we once found an active beehive in a closet, and of course, there was that time we discovered a man living in a car in the backyard. I thought I was ready for anything. But Bessie Smith and crashing piano chords?

Dad asked, "Do you have the owner's number?"

In the end, we called the realty office and asked them to come out. The agent was armed with bug spray and cleaning supplies, but there's little you can do with the blues. He probably thought we were nuts.

Mom and Dad left on Thursday morning, glad to be away from the tune. My sister smudged the porch, and my brother-in-law bought a Bessie Smith retrospective and tried to educate the rest of us that evening.

A month later, the owner sent me a nice thank you note and our deposit. He said nothing about the piano or the song. My son still hums a little Bessie when he wants to remind me of that vacation. Sometimes it doesn't matter if you get rid of the piano, the ghosts are just part of the place.

Blessing the Bakery of the Saints

I

After the elder Mr. Winston died last January, Alberta Saint Pierre baked intricate recipes earlier and earlier in the morning. She glanced at the wall clock—4 A.M. The hush of early morning met the rush of rain pounding through the rainspouts and pouring through the center of the alley. Though the kitchen door was locked, the dampness of the spring storm crept into the room and lurked in moisture hanging in the air which affected the recipe for pie crust, pastry, and meringue.

Pausing to stretch, she caught her distorted reflection in the shining range hood where lemon filling cooled, and the beginning of custard waited for her attention. Her long, fine braids twisted back and tucked under a white slouched cap, Berta twitched her nose but did not wipe her face with flour-dusted, dark hands. Berta observed the oval shape of her smooth, dark face, the whites of large brown eyes and approved her serious mouth. Smiles were reserved for customers since opening the bakery five years ago.

Berta wiped her hands on the damp towel she used over the dough and frowned at the rain pouring over the clogged downspout of the business across the alley from hers. All her time was devoted to the myriad needs of the bakery business, its building, the customers, and her employees. Since Mr. Winston's death, she factored in time for her new partner—an encumbrance through an unpaid debt.

From nine to closing at six, George, old Mr. Winston's son and the heir to her debt, offered his opinions, shared his penny-pinching worries, and fouled the sweet air around the pastry table with his sour talk about money. Berta pretended to listen to her new business partner but found excuses not to discuss anything with George. She did watch him like a hunted creature; he towered over her though she was no tiny woman, and the frown between his eyes gave him a vulture-like hunch when his diatribes on expenses were met with silence. Once he had taken the stool no one used and lowered his big frame to watch her decorate cupcakes for a catered party. His eyes were lighter brown than hers and striated with green which gave him a predatory look like a prowling, sleek cat. He used something on his curly, dark hair that emitted a lemony scent. Berta closed her eyes and considered lemon meringue for the special next week.

Berta's day assistant giggled when she spoke to George Winston and often teased Berta about him hanging about in the office early and late. "Doesn't he have his own business to run, Berta? Stop ignoring him. You treat that man like a gnat!" Her day assistant, a neighborhood abuelita with a fondness for romance, grinned when she chided Berta but rolled out flaky pie crusts that had customers ordering the deep-dish southern desserts for every holiday and family dinner. Berta rolled her eyes—George usually left to drive across town to his company an hour after the pie crust was prepared and the usual morning rush of customers had dwindled. Her day assistant was fond of the big man through limited exposure to his suave manner with the customers, not deep ramblings on the cost of ingredients or the quotes she'd gathered for new equipment.

Her morning helper Trevion arrived at six a.m. to work a few hours before school. He usually wrapped a few catering orders, filched a muffin for his breakfast, and started the coffee

urns. He opened the place for business when the first customers tried the door at seven. At eight-thirty, he would pick up
his backpack and jog toward the avenue where he caught the
public bus to school. Alberta would watch him leave and bite
her lip. Three months after old Mr. Winston's death, Trevion
left earlier each day to avoid speaking to George Winston, who
arrived promptly at eight.

George had first met the boy at old Mr. Winston's funeral.
George had taken one look at the boy's short dreads, the freck-
les sprinkled across his coffee-colored complexion, and asked,
"You work for Berta every day? I hope you wear a hairnet at
the bakery."

Trevion had tossed back his brown and orange-tipped spires
that spiked out all over a well-formed head. He narrowed his
large eyes and snarled, "Sure thing, sir. And Ms. Saint Pierre's
name is said, 'Bear-Ta' not 'Bur-tah' like she's American."

Berta often studied the boy as he worked. Trevion's beautiful deep brown eyes observed like she, did but his smile was
easier. He bristled when he spoke to George Winston. Trevion started audacious humming whenever George tried to step
into the kitchen. George would arch one crisp, black eyebrow,
smooth down his tie, or tug at the bottom edge of his suit jacket,
but shuffle away. Trevion had almost gotten himself fired when
he sprinkled George's sleeve with powdered sugar one morning.
Making it worse by trying to dust it off, he blundered by mut-
tering, "What fool would wear a black suit into a bakery?"

George had bellowed, "Stop that. You know I go on to the
office every day. Not everyone spends the day making desserts,
you know." The man and the boy rubbed each other like two
grades of sandpaper—fine and coarse—and wore her morning thin.

By March, Berta and George had fallen into a grudge-match

over expenses versus improvements to the bakery. He admitted ignorance about food service, but he insisted repeatedly that he had made a fortune in fasteners. Berta listened to one side of his business calls and imagined hills of bright copper rings and silver snaps piled in a dark warehouse.

George's father had been Berta's silent partner—the only source of cash she could find when the original owners, an old Greek couple, asked Berta to buy them out five years ago. She had tried for a loan at the neighborhood bank, but the stiff-faced woman behind the loan officer's desk had looked cold-eyed at Berta's business plan. The bank sent a short, insulting note about risk and lack of collateral. Berta's grandmother had suggested asking Mr. Winston for the money—he ran the corner bar at the end of their street, drove a nice car, and was known for lending small sums between paychecks.

Mr. Winston only asked Berta for payments on the loan when he needed extra cash. The old man had visited once every few months for a bag of pastries or a pie, and a fistful of cash that Berta kept in a rubber band, locked in the old safe under her desk. She had not bargained to inherit the man's son at Mr. Winston's death. She had attended the old man's funeral surrounded by the bakery staff and had half-expected a note forgiving the balance, but paperwork was produced that showed that the loan balance had grown into a few thousand more than she figured. George Winston had come to clear his father's possessions out of the family home, and in turn, to micromanage her bakery among his father's other business interests. He had sold the bar months ago, invested more funds into the neighborhood cleaners, and was well-received by the old couple who ran a variety store a few blocks away on the avenue. Only Berta accepted his attention with distrust.

George Winston plagued her with his daily presence. Ber-

ta daydreamed about abandoning the bakery on the corner of
Conkling and Read. The old people would miss her until another cook was located. She imagined the windows dark and
the showcases empty, the ovens cold, and dust instead of sugar,
butter and flour smells permeating the building. Berta squinted
over rolling dough that morning and began to pray for a miracle.

Berta's mind wandered as her hands crafted, cajoled, and
pressed the raw ingredients into tempting wares for the showcases. Smear-case for the old folks, as well as iced tarts, pecan
twirls, sticky walnut buns, and small pies with lattice tops that
revealed the filling cradled inside. Danish, alone, took an hour
to produce—standbys like prune and cherry, a few peach for the
old men, chocolate for the housewives and lemon for luck. Her
day assistant started the full-size pies when she arrived at ten.
Pies and cakes were baked on demand with the daily features
sold by the slice packaged the evening before and managed with
a huge checklist that Berta had created the week she opened the
place as the Saint Pierre Patisserie of Highlandtown.

Praying for a miracle set off a warp of memory. Berta's first
visited this bakery as a child with her grandmother. The small
corner bakery was one block off the main thoroughfare and op-
posite the old Catholic church. In her youth, the business had
been surrounded by a lawyers' office, a confectionary, a pizza
take-out joint, and the Democratic Club. By the time she had
taken a loan with Mr. Winston, her elder neighbor and confi-
dante, the law office had moved, the candy shop had closed, the
pizza place was still open, and the Democratic Club had been
replaced by a bail bondsman. The Luna Bakery served as an an-
chor for the neighborhood— owned by the old Greek couple,
it took up the space of three row houses. Berta remembered
standing in front of the showcase with cheesecake and crumb
cake just like she still offered and her grandmother hissing, "Al-

ways look at the floors, Alberta. If the place is clean, it's safe to buy." A bit louder because it was part of the act, the old lady continued, "That white place off of Edmondson is dirty—everything from that place tastes like Lysol." Berta smiled thinking about her grandmother who had developed cancer soon after and lingered for years in the small upstairs bedroom, too weak to do much more than dream and moan.

When Berta had been nine, she took over the chore of shopping with the old woman who moved to the United States to marry her brother's friend—a good-looking Haitian man who worked in the steel mill. Husband long dead, Grand'Mere Lucy stayed in the small bedroom at the top of the stairs in the old house and watched the children until they had to watch out for her. Berta smiled as she remembered her grandmother's rambling lectures as they walked up to the Avenue and bought from each vendor much like Berta still preferred to do.

Berta ignored those who assumed she was "right off the boat" with her gentle, rolling accent that lapsed into the broken French that had been spoken in her house. Her speech gave away her heritage, but she refused, even during the heady days of culinary school, to force the lilt completely out of her voice. The soothing cadence of island sounds outlasted outside pressures.

The rain had slackened and then returned by the time Berta finished the Danish trays and shoved them into the oven. Trevion unlocked the front door with a priest in tow. "Hey, Miss Berta? The priest wants to see you."

Berta blushed thinking about her failure to attend services but praying while she baked. Filling the orders for the Sunday coffee clutches had been her way to serve for years. The old pastor of the church across the street had asked her a few weeks ago if she was Catholic—"So many of your people are devout Catholics. You should attend a service some time." She had considered giving the pastor what her mother called a "hairy eyeball" when he said it. Instead she reigned herself in like she'd been trained, dutiful daughter, fine student, and business woman.

Berta cast an eye down to her apron and beige kitchen trousers. She brushed herself off and thrust her shoulders back to speak to the old pastor. Pushing through the double doors that separated the kitchen from the shop, Berta stopped at the sight of a man dressed in black, who was pushing damp hair off his face. He was a regular customer with whom she traded jokes, observations, and compliments. She had built a few fantasies around his visits. Medium height with wide-set shoulders, this customer usually wore a dark warm-up suit that contrasted his shock of reddish brown hair. He was damp from the rain but her eyes were drawn to his collar—the white collar of a minister or priest.

He smiled at her shock and murmured, "Good morning. I hate to disrupt your work, Berta, but could you come across the street and help me with Father Alphonse?"

Behind him came in two elderly men with their wet coats, glistening fedoras covered with plastic, toothy smiles, and fogged glasses. They chorused, "Good morning, Miss Saint Pierre." Berta smiled toward the customers and motioned to Trevion to take their orders. She turned back to the priest who shifted away from the customers' curious glances.

The priest reminded her of Claude Raines from long ago movies she watched with her grandmother—Raines had been a handsome man but cold. This version had a twinkle in his eye though his face was wet. It had been raining all morning; everything in the bakery felt wet. She stared at him. His hair was sparkling wet with the rain. As she stood silent, he sobered into worry. He said, "Berta, I've come for a favor." He smiled gently with no more foolishness. He said, "Yes, I know you don't know me well, but I need someone to vouch for me."

Blinking over the request, Berta repeated the word, "Vouch?" Her experience with the word was limited to matters of vows, promises, and broken contracts. Berta moved behind the pastry case and leaned in to take a cinnamon muffin off the second glass shelf. She offered it to the priest. She said, "All I know is what you have for breakfast. I know that you come almost every day." She eyed him and thought about old Mr. Winston who lent her money when no one else would. She reached behind her back to untie her apron, Berta said, "I will speak for you."

"Please come with me now." He placed the muffin on the counter and withdrew a few bills, handing them to Trevion.

The boy tossed back his head and asked, "Don't you want coffee, Padre?"

The door opened and a single buffet from the wet draft brushed over the threshold. Shaking his umbrella, George Winston entered. He glanced at the assembly and took off his raincoat which dripped all over the floor. "Good morning. Trevion, we'll need a mop up here."

Berta burst out, "You're early."

The priest frowned at the drops of water on the floor, the customers, and Trevion. Berta handed her apron to George and said, "I'm going with the priest. Take out the Danish trays in ten minutes and the cakes in thirty." She turned to Trevion. "Stay here until I return. Do you understand? I know you don't have class till 9:30. Help Mr. Winston for me." She didn't wait for Trevion or George to agree. She took George's long raincoat from the hook and swept out the door of bakery as another passel of customers arrived.

They crossed the rain-slicked street side-by-side. At the sidewalk before the steps to the large double doors to the church, Berta looked up to the priest and asked, "What is your name?"

The man's cheeks and forehead were rosy. He fumbled over it, "Pastor . . . Charles . . . well, most folks call me 'Charlie' around the parish."

"Not this parish." Berta's eyes narrowed as she thought about his appearances in the bakery, the running clothes, the snatched breakfast, his glib jokes, and little compliments. "What do you want from Father Alphonse?"

His eyes darted toward the massive oaken doors. He leaned a bit closer to murmur over the sound of the traffic and the rain, "I need a miracle."

Berta huffed out half a laugh and nodded. "Don't we all, sir?"

II

The church with its conjoined rectory squatted in a half a city block and dominated the neighborhood. Built in 1895, a thin crust of pollution had yellowed the white marble doorway and dulled the grey granite façade, muting the magnificence of the building. Berta climbed the steps to the main entry doors of Saint Elizabeth of Hungary. She glanced back at Pastor Charlie as he started to speak. He gave a lopsided grin then said, "Each of these old churches were founded by different ethnic groups as they immigrated. Casimir's was for the Polish."

Berta nodded. "My family attended the Italian church—Pompeii. It's closer to my house." The inside of this Gothic-style church was painted and carpeted in the manner of thirty years past—the cardinal red of the last resurgence of the faith during the seventies. Berta glanced at the floors and noticed the haze of poorly-removed cleansers. She peered around in the silent, darkened entryway and remembered it lit with overhead lanterns and noisy with the echoing murmur of parishioners before services. The weekday hush of disuse permeated the building.

Pastor Charlie led Berta to a narrow doorway beyond the confessionals where they entered the hallway that led to the parish offices and rectory. Berta had seldom ventured into the rectory though she donated weekly platters for the priests and the Sunday social.

They skirted past an empty reception desk. Berta followed the broad back of the priest, as he strode down a hallway lit by intermittent sconces. Without hesitation, he turned and passed through another doorway into the pastor's office on the right.

Berta had visited the church office once before—after her grandmother died. Berta's mother wanted the funeral mass at this grand church instead of the small neighborhood one they attended during the holidays. Father Alphonse had granted Berta's request that day with the understanding that she would join the parish. Berta blushed as guilt over reneging on the full intention of that promise. The plates of pastries, the cakes, and pies she donated every week had attended in her absence. She was on the parish rolls—she mailed her contribution monthly just like she sent a check to her cousins in Jacmel. Berta had never met her island-bound cousins, and she had rarely attended services at the big church a few blocks from her bakery. She hovered in the doorway to the Pastor Alphonse's office.

Due to the sparse light from floor lamps, the large room was shadowed. Berta peered at the old man seated behind a large desk. Behind him, a double window was covered with deep red, velvet curtains. The dark wood, the gloom of the day and the cardinal red of this interior were nightmarish. Berta's mind flashed back to the bakery—she yearned for the overhead lights, the warmth, the smells of baking, the chorus of greetings from customers, even George's comments, and Trevion's sniping. She stepped forward and frowned at the hunched figure seated behind the desk.

She looked at Pastor Charlie who was talking, though she

had not been paying attention to the content of his rushed speech. He was asking, imploring the old pastor who stared down at his desk blotter and said nothing. Berta interrupted, "Father Alphonse? Are you sick?"

She jumped when the old man sat back and glared at her. He asked, "Have you come here to beg forgiveness for your sins?" His eyes were glassy and unseeing.

Berta scolded, "No. Father Alphonse." She took a breath and spoke again, "I've come to beg you to listen to this man. He says he needs your help."

The old priest burst out with a laugh. "Help? He wants to take Saint Elizabeth with him. You, Alberta Saint Pierre—Berta from the Bakery of the Saints—how could you come here to help a thief?"

Berta blew an impatient gush through her lips. "That's Saint Pierre—my name." She shook her head at the moniker thrust upon the business that was more hard work than she had ever expected. Berta glanced back to the other man and asked, "How can you take the church? What nonsense are you both talking about?" Her pocket began to buzz, so she withdrew the cell phone she had forgotten. "Excuse me," she murmured, stepped back, and turned to go out into the hallway.

Before she could put phone back to her ear, the two priests began to bicker. A terse voice erupted in her ear. George's voice boomed through the stark distance between the bakery and the parish office. "Berta! Where are you?"

"St. Elizabeth's." The sounds of the two men shouting at each other echoed in the empty hallway. Berta moved away from the office.

George asked, "Is there trouble?"

Berta rolled her eyes but gasped as Pastor Charlie burst out of the office and stomped past her toward the main part of the church. She followed him at a little distance and slowed midway through the pews. She said softly into the phone, "George? I'll be back soon. Take the pastries out and remove them from the pan. Gently." She snapped the phone shut and watched the pastor try to reach the wall sconce near the sacristy by climbing onto a chair and stretching one great arm over his head.

Rushing forward, Berta asked though her voice echoed throughout the cavernous room, "Are you stealing something?"

He reached the sconce, opened the small door and felt around inside the vessel. He turned and shouted in a harsh grating sound that reverberated around the altar, "There's nothing in there." Berta stood confused at the old altar railing—what had he expected? Pastor Charlie rushed back through the sacristy toward the hallway and the pastor's office.

Berta followed him slowly—a shiver had crawled across her back as if someone had touched her, a light touch from an unseen hand. She uttered a little prayer her grandmother used to say, "Jezi O, padone peche nou, sove n anba dife lanfè . . ." She broke off as she crossed the threshold from the cold hallway to the pastor's silent office.

The pastor stepped up to the desk. His fists were clenched. "It's not for me. I am asking for a little girl—a child who believes St. Elizabeth has a miracle for her."

Father Alphonse scoffed, "You Lutherans don't believe in the saints."

"My niece believes in your Saint Elizabeth. She attended your feast day service with her best friend. She heard your homily and the litany of miracles attributed to her—saint of the poor, the sick . . . and bakers." Charlie stumbled over the words as he glanced back at Berta.

Father Alphonse was nodding. His fist trembled where it rested on his desk blotter.

Pastor Charlie added, "The intercession of the saint is all I seek. We are arguing semantics while my niece is going into surgery at eight with or without her miracle." He turned back to Berta and clasped his hands as if in prayer. "Try to intercede for me, Berta. I am just borrowing Saint Elizabeth for a few hours."

Berta felt her blood grow cold as a shiver swept her again. Borrow the saint? The old priest began to cough, and Berta looked around for a glass of water for him. She said, "I'm getting you a drink, Father Alphonse."

She fled down the hall to the rectory kitchen where the woman who volunteered to keep house for the pastor was drinking tea at the sink. "Good morning. The pastor needs water or coffee."

The older woman produced a mug and filled it with coffee. She said, "He hasn't been feeling well."

Berta said, "I'll take it to him." She glanced at her watch thinking of George and Trevion in the bakery—the trays of tarts burned, the customers standing at the counter in confusion. She hurried up the hallway and thought she heard the murmur of men's voices inside the church.

Inside the office, Berta found Father Alphonse, still sitting but frozen in his seat with his eyes wide open. Placing the mug on the desk, she knelt beside him and checked his pulse. His limp arm fell heavily as she grasped at his hand. Inside his palm lay a narrow vessel of beveled glass. Its top and bottom were encased in filigreed gold. Berta caught it as it fell out of his hand. Father Alphonse listed to the side—almost falling out of the chair. She palmed the little vessel and eased the priest back to slump with his head resting on his desk. She could not bring herself to close his eyes as she had done for her grandmother.

As the volume of the argument at the door to the rectory rose, the housekeeper bustled past the door. She glanced toward Berta with a shrug, but she did not noticed Father Alphonse. Choking over calling out to the housekeeper, Berta straightened to standing beside the desk. She held the small container up to the desk lamp and examined the thin fragment that looked more like a spent cigarette than the finger of the revered saint. "Hello, Elizabeth, patron saint of bakers," she whispered to the bit of tissue and bone in the reliquary. Her mind flew to the miracles she'd wished for that morning, and she caught herself hoping for one with the fervency of a child. She clutched the saint in her palm like Alphonse had and closed her eyes. "Help me, Saint Elizabeth. Show me the way." Her heart grew ponderously heavy, and the vessel burned in her hand. She sucked in a breath, surprised at the faint scent of vanilla, cinnamon, and warmed butter wafting through the doorway. She clutched at the desk to steady herself.

On the desktop was a letter from the archbishop. She scanned it without hesitation as men's voices could be heard moving through the church along with protests from the housekeeper. The archbishop gave permission for Reverend Charles Raines to take the reliquary of St. Elizabeth to his niece. The little girl had written a letter to the Pope in Rome asking for this favor. Why had Father Alphonse been so stubborn? Berta's eyes fled back to the old man's blank stare.

Tears had obscured her vision when two policemen, Reverend Charlie, and George Winston invaded the room. The housekeeper followed and cried out when she saw the condition of Father Alphonse. Everyone spoke at once, but Berta gave the letter to one of the policemen and showed him the reliquary.

Berta offered Pastor Charlie the reliquary in an open palm. "You should go to your niece. Do you have your car?" Father Charlie rushed through giving his information and producing his copy of the letter from the archbishop. He was whisked away by the older of the two policeman.

The younger officer called the morgue after checking

the old priest's pulse. "He's cold but limp. Probably dead for some time."

George had come to stand beside Berta. He placed an arm about her shoulders. Berta shook her head. She said, "I just spoke to him." George's hold tightened.

The young policeman shrugged. "I know what you think you saw, but the old guy has been gone for a while." He looked down into Berta's eyes and said quietly, "My grandfather would say it was Saint Elizabeth." He glanced around the cluttered office and frowned. "Only a few of these old churches still have the bones of the saints. The old folks tell stories about miracles."

Berta trembled, and George asked, "May we go?" The policeman nodded.

Instead of exiting, Berta entered the church and walked up the side aisle. Berta took a step toward the saint's alcove in the shadow of the Blessed Mother. The porcelain, the paint cracked in faded blues, rose, and highlighted with gold, reminded Berta of the pastries she had left baking. She turned to George and asked, "The pastries. Tell me you took them out of the oven." At the crestfallen look on his face, she uttered, "Sorry. I'm so sorry."

His voice roughened as he admitted, "When you left this morning, I, well, your customers asked after you. They were worried about you—their island girl—they said they call you."

Berta nodded. The gentle teasing from the old men was expected—they didn't know how to relate to the diverse populations migrating into their old neighborhood. Berta had been born at the city hospital like most of their grandchildren, but to them she was the little Creole girl whose people had lived in Haiti and spoke in the gentle cadence of the warmer climate. Their neighbors from Mexico spoke their soft language in rapid, machine gun vivacity. The blacks had their own subterfuge of plain English and jargon sometimes put on to confuse. Berta grumbled as she stood beside George, "I'm as American as they are." Again, her eyes fled back to Saint Elizabeth and then to the statue of the Virgin holding her baby.

George smiled at the soft "tay-er" that her accent produced. He nodded. "Yes, you are, Alberta." He said her name correctly, and it forced her eyes back to him. He continued, "And you are an excellent businesswoman. When you left this morning, Trevion told me that I make you miserable. He told me that you want to fight me, but that it is not in your nature." He chuckled and added, "That boy is devoted to you, Berta. All the time we were taking care of your blessed trays, he was telling me off."

Alberta looked up into George Winston's face and tried to see him clearly in the half-light. A mistaken haze of irritation lifted, and she saw the man who managed his business by phone in order to hang around the old neighborhood longer than he should have after his father's death. He was taller than his father, but old Mr. Winston had shrunken from years tending bar and doling out loans. His black hair was tightly curled and cropped where his father's had been shaved clean during the end of his life. Berta saw the marks from flour or powdered sugar on George's cuffs. His shoulders were square-set and broad, yet he was trimly narrow through the hips. She asked, "Were your people Nigerian?"

He smiled. Then he shrugged and said, "My mother always said so, but I think that was all mumbo-jumbo that came out of the sixties. It's a wonder she didn't do the whole—back to Africa thing."

"You look like a prince." She cast down her eyes. "What do you want, George?"

"I want you to see me as more than an enemy, Alberta." They both looked back as the medical examiner arrived and bustled down the hallway from the church entrance. George held out a hand. He asked, "What do you want, Alberta Saint Pierre?"

She took his hand and started to walk down the aisle toward the door, the rainy sidewalk, and her bakery. His hand was warm, and she squeezed it before she answered, "I want a miracle, George Winston."

Mayday. Mayday. Mayday.

We were simply out for an after-dinner boat ride. The breeze had picked up since noon, but it was still less than 10 knots. There was a slight chop as we left the creek which made the water look like chunky, gray tiles. One other craft was ambling away from our cove, but it was a larger boat—a tri-hull with a great big Johnson twin-prop engine. You shouted all that about the other boat over the noise of our smaller, older one. I knew our outboard was a Johnson, too, because I'd bought it three boats ago to power the dingy we kept for the 40-foot sailboat. The sailboat? I sold it after the divorce, after all the squabbles over nothing.

We rounded the corner around the sandbar and hit the opening in the river that is wide enough to name it Norman's Creek. The engine sounded as if it was struggling to carry us beyond the piers and into the main channel. I looked back at you and saw your jaw tighten. Was it tension or a lean into this challenge? I trained my eye on the channel marker. We had run aground too many times in our deep-keel 40-foot not to have earned some respect for markers. I turned back to you and mimed, "Don't cut it too close."

You glared at me and rolled your shoulders a smidge. So, it was the challenge. You twisted the choke, and the engine whirred into power. I automatically turned my head to stare at the marina signs warning about minding your wake. The chop was fiercer than any wake we could churn. You were scowling. The other boat had made it to the channel buoy and eased into a slight curve to the right and the wider Middle Branch. The setting sun reflected off its sides in the hazy orange painted closer to the horizon.

In another few minutes, we reached the same point and met the main channel in a spray that drenched the forward seats. I was momentarily glad we left the dog on the pier and that none of the kids had been visiting. The dampness of the spray penetrated my light jacket. I dared myself not to look back at you. I imagined you smiting me with a glance if I turned and begged off or suggested a calmer tack back into one of the side creeks.

All I'd said over dinner was, "Remember we used to go for drinks at Whitey and Dots back in the day?" I'd been sipping coffee and looking out at the sunset on the river. The sky was painted those dazzling oranges and reds of spring that were so often pinks and purples in winter. I missed the old days of winter sunsets reflected on the protected creek as calm as a painted rock. I missed the easier days of the bigger boats and the endless cash to spend when we wanted. But then your Dad left us, and the big boat was sold, and we scrimped and saved where we could.

I was left with this surly man you turned out to be. You are just like your dad despite all those efforts to break out of the mold with the desk job and dress clothes. When I catch you staring at me like that, he is back with all that condescension, all that damning attitude toward anything female. Or simply me.

Instead of heading perpendicular to the channel buoy, you steered the boat toward the bay. Glancing back, I saw you frowning but not at me. Your eye was trained ahead—out to the island instead of across the Middle Branch to our destination—the waterfront bar in the far cove. You were steering into the arc that would take us out into rougher water than we'd ever taken this glorified rowboat. You pointed and I stared into the wind toward the island. A thin trail of smoke streamed from a brighter orange flame ahead into an increasingly darker gray chop of ruffled water. The boat we followed out of the cove was on fire.

I reached beneath the brief console and touched the switch for the radio. "Mayday. Mayday. Mayday. Boat fire off Turkey Point on the Middle Branch. Home port Norman's Creek. Mayday. Mayday. Mayday."

You shouted over the noise. "Take over, Mom?"

I nodded.

Celia's Audience with a Madman

1

"Doctor Tregoning?" Nothing answered but the hum of generators thrumming in the background. Despite the deep, velvet black, Celia sensed there was something else in the room with her. Then a scrim of electricity vibrated above her like a batwing and prickled the skin on her arms. Even before her hair rose to greet the static created by the creature's twisting appendages, she noticed the quiver in her eyelashes and her fine brow hairs. The minute down on her arms rose—every feather of her being rushed to encounter his.

Slowly, sensors lit and hovered before her and in her periphery. The depth of the room was shrouded in darkness, but myriad jointed arms extended to greet her. Celia knew the creature before she gave him a name. She had seen the drawings and typed up the narratives from the scribbles surrounding the schematics. One night she had unearthed her brother's battered collection of comic books after translating the engineer's drawings all day. Celia remembered rolling her eyes at the fantasy aspect, but she could grasp the theoretical beginnings of it.

"Hello?" She took a step forward and felt the extensions recoil. Her supervisor had blathered about robots replacing human workers when he labored past exhaustion and drank from the bottle in his desk. The company wanted an untiring, self-sufficient workforce capable of twenty-four hour-a-day production. She blinked into the sensors poised at eye-level—here it was.

"Doctor Tregoning? It's Celia Maycomb." Celia wanted to roll her eyes at the selfishness of the company accountants promoted to the president's office at the rural chicken processing plant. How many more chicken farms were needed to support such an endeavor? A job was a job, and that was her reason for working for at the plant that belched an acrid, mealy odor over her little town. Her lip curled.

More lights on other appendages engaged and lit up the room at floor level. This robot was the most complex she had ever seen. Of course, there were small areas of the plant that were mechanized, but each machine needed the human overseer or rendered product ready for human assembly.

This creature might be the product of the research manifestos that she had massaged into a few bound manuals only her boss, the lead engineer, kept in a locked file drawer. Her knowledge from the reports could not be discounted—they had trusted her to keep their secrets. She had signed the non-disclosure agreements and then scribed each file for the private archives kept for future consideration. How much cyber-thieving was there in this particular business? Was there truly the threat of intellectual piracy among the chicken nugget manufacturers of the world? She had categorized the research, the lab experiments and their results as wild, cerebral driveling. Dr. Drew Tregoning, her immediate boss and one of the most prolific engineers of the Castro Department, channeled the mad scientist at times.

Celia mentally shook her head to toss out all prior knowledge and misinformation. She had automatically craned her neck, arched her back slightly and widened her eyes though instinct cautioned hunching her body into protection of soft tissue like the eyes, cheeks, and softly parted lips. She closed her mouth the moment she noticed her image in the monitor attached to the wall across from the door she had entered moments ago. She had simply pressed on the previously hidden door, crossed the threshold with no alarm sounding, and closed it with a surreptitious tug. Inside the cavernous, dark room, she wondered why she had gained entry with so little effort.

The blank, gray door at the end of the long hallway which ended her floor's suite of offices had tempted her during her first week at the plant. No doorknob, no plaque like the rest of the series of locked doors, and no one venturing in or out. A closet? A sealed area? When she first examined the door there hadn't been scratch marks on the sill—marks that originated from the other side. Now ominous gouges marked the wood threshold, and a slug-like trail gleamed from the door and ended in the middle of the cavernous room.

Months ago, Tregoning had given Celia a lengthy journal that might have birthed this creature hovering and whirring right above her head. The glut of work had distracted her during the entire ninety-day trial period for new employees and had lulled her into entertained complacence. The essays were sometimes lab notes written out in paragraphs that sounded like monologues as she typed and edited. The work was focused on robotics and the possibility of a fully automated plant that could repair itself as parts jammed, broke, or malfunctioned. The historic malfunctions described were often labeled the "human element" because, simply put, human beings are not dependable when under pressure. Machines were more efficient.

Four nights ago, Tregoning had disappeared down the hallway and had not reemerged. Celia had silently scoffed when one of the other supervisors mentioned that Drew Tregoning was extending his stay in Caribbean for a tech conference. There was no tech conference in the Caribbean or anywhere between the doctor's walk past her cubicle one evening and his complete vaporization. She mused that there should never be lies in research—just fact piled onto fact in a ponderous line that sequentially told a story, solved a problem, or equated into some truth. Research created something like this fantastic creature tumbling and whirring its extensions fast enough to maintain a static charge in the air around her person.

Celia blinked out of theory and mute perusal when she saw herself on a monitor. What was this thing? A prototype? A plaything? A pretend vacation from reality? There was one optical extension poised an arm-length from her face, but the monitor showed her from many angles, so she concluded that there were many more lenses. The zoom hovered close and then backed away. The picture on the screen broke into multiple images—one in three dimensions and in another, a thermal reading in which her body was shaded a surreal, fuzzy green-blue swirled with tinges of red in the face, chest and belly. Numbers ran in a ticker down the screen at the right edge that she assumed were respiration, heart rate, and temperature. Some of the numbers were stated in algorithms that begged her to study. Celia opened and closed her eyes to break out of the short stasis with which wonder petrified her.

"My name is Celia Maycomb." The arms danced in reaction, and Celia's hair rose in silvery-blond strands of attention from her scalp. She resisted the urge to smooth them down. As a rule of thumb, she made no fast moves on barking dogs, angry men, or curious scientific experiments. That thought quirked her lips.

A voice boomed, "Cecelia Jane Maycomb. Office C42, Department Castro. No clearance." Unconsciously, Celia's shoulders drooped a bit. The voice was tinny and flat. She continued to gaze upward and count extensions—seven which stopped at a uniform distance from her and took readings and adjusted in a quick-motion jerkiness. When she imagined such a creature, the appendages moved smoothly, and the processing was instantaneous.

Celia rolled her eyes at the automaton. "The door opened the moment I touched it. And only my mother calls me Cecelia. I'll leave you alone then." She turned toward the door and felt the first prickle of fear course up her spine. The door had disappeared, and another monitor had taken its place. Seven appendages surrounded her while warning computations arced through her brain: optical, taste, tactile, olfactory, and auditory. What else? Temperature, perhaps? What other sensory device would she design for such a creature? There had been one odd study on extrasensory perception that had been out of step with the rest of research on bees, the human nervous system, artificial intelligence, and fusion models.

The voice spoke right into her ear and made her start. "Celia Maycomb. Clearance granted. Stay." The tumble of arms pulling back had her stepping toward them. The blinks of tiny bulbs in one drew her to lean in to see it better. Booming, the voice warned, "Do not touch. Touch hurts."

Celia nodded as her eyes widened at the possibilities. "I work with Drew Tregoning. Where is he?" The clicks above her buzzed in a hive of processing. She counted on her fingers before it answered. Processing was slowed to seconds when saving new information. In her periphery, the optic monitor showed the quiver of her fingers keeping track of the moments. She stilled her fingers. The machine was studying her reactions. She had edited Tregoning's essay on the revelations of eye blinks, lid movement, and other facial muscle contraction. He had unlocked the secrets of the iris which she had found interesting, if speculative. Had he taught the creature the same methods of divining human intention? "What foolishness," she muttered.

"Touch hurts," the voice intoned. Then the tone shifted toward conclusion, "Touch hurts humans." Silence followed the declaration.

Celia slowed her breathing, and her hair descended from its ascent chasing electrocution. She made her eyes remain steady and steely. She looked straight into the monitor because it was human to look at the appendages of a strange creature and fail to look it in the eye. "I won't touch you then. Where is Drew Tregoning?" She held her breath then panted a bit to throw off the parts tracking her expulsion of carbon dioxide. She immediately felt a breath of air brush by her arm as some unseen air duct opened.

"Follow the light." The finality of the blank voice struck her. A cold lump of fear lodged in her throat. Curiosity had delivered her through the gray door at the end of the hallway on her own floor. Curiosity vanquished; all Celia truly desired was escape. She turned toward the series of spotlights that bounced off the dull, gray floor and allowed her feet to move her. Perhaps there was an exit like the glowing red sign under the screen at the theater that beaconed release from danger.

Before she reached the dark square at the far end of the warehouse-sized expanse, she asked the creature one more question, "Did his touch hurt you?"

"You." The word baffled it.

"What does the creator call you? What is your name?" Dimly in the gloom of the dark warehouse, she saw a form on a bed about thirty feet away. As she continued forward, she noted that he was sprawled limply either in sleep or death. When she was less than ten feet from the bed, she saw vitals displayed on the smaller monitor that displayed numbers that revealed shallow respiration and a very slow heart rate. Could a human survive under thirty beats per minute? Brain activity—the seventh appendage must be for brain activity because a very faint grey pulse beat in the scanned creature's head. Hers had been red and swirling—perhaps it hadn't been a simple thermal image but a combination of thermals, brain activity, and body functions.

Again, the processing time lengthened with the new query, her movement, and unguarded concern for the man inert on the bare mattress. As she bent to touch the doctor, the creature boomed, "Touch hurts."

Celia straightened and frowned at the twitching arms that hesitated to pull her back from their pet. She shook her head, "Humans touch each other. Touch does not always hurt." She sighed and took another breath for patience. "Something went wrong when he touched you."

"Do not touch. Touch hurts." The appendages crowded between Celia and Tregoning.

She cast her mind to distracting it. "What is your name?" She nearly stamped her foot in a burst of impatience to scare the creature away like a wild animal.

"Serial number LX, Floor Castro."

She cocked her head and thought about their dilemma. The man on the bed released a huge sigh and made her impulsive, "LX? As in sixty in Latin? How about Alex? Alex Castro, if you want a last name." The man on the bed turned his head toward her voice and groaned.

Celia lowered herself to squatting by the mattress-like platform. She peered at the limp body of the man and the stage on which he was draped. The bed was not a mattress but a raised box of some sort that kept Tregoning off the cement floor about three feet. Cold emanated from the gray, dull surface of the unfinished cement.

The doctor's whiskers looked grown out a few days but

not the nearly four he'd been missing. The rest of his face was the milk-gray of oatmeal, and the odor of scorched cotton hung about him. Celia wondered if that spoke of partial electrocution.

Sweet. Celia had never been irritated enough with the man to wish him harm, but others in the department had poked fun at his wild theories behind his back. Drew Tregoning was "going tres mad," one of the assistants had mocked. This man looked as if he had been twisted into a knot and dropped on the platform. She leaned over to observe without touching him as the creature's arms flashed in her periphery. His fingertips on the exposed right hand were blistered as if burned, and his socks looked oddly worn through just on the bottoms. What had happened? Malfunction? Program error?

The man who used to be Dr. Andrew Tregoning, the mad theorist and condescending genius of the Castro Division, moved his head and opened bloodshot eyes. They narrowed to distress and instant alarm. "Maycomb?" His voice croaked from disuse, "Leave."

The creature's arms whirled and dipped faster. Celia felt her hair make contact with one flailing appendage and sizzle in a flash of tinder and then crumble. "Doctor! Hush!" She cast an eye to the other arms that might crowd her if she didn't control panic. She summoned up anger, "Stay back, Alex. Touch hurts. Do not touch me."

She sucked in a breath and ignored the man who had rolled over and lay with his eyes wide and panicked. How long had he been rendered insensible by the creature through an inadvertent touch? She opened and closed her eyes. She focused on the extended arm of the centipede-like optical probe with its hundreds of tiny camera lens. The monitor was flashing a dizzying ballet of dueling images featuring two beings. "Doctor? Alex allowed me to enter the lab. Alex is concerned about your condition."

"Alex?" She watched the doctor recover full-consciousness though his eyes reflected the blended images of LX's probes recording every nuance of her lion-like appearance with the extended froth of long, gold and silver hair and enormous amber-flecked, green eyes. He blinked up at her in shock, but then his eyes narrowed on her purposeful widening and narrowing eyes. She tried Morse Code to goad him into movement. Her mouth curved into a smirk as she abandoned the message "M-O-V-E." She blinked more boldly, G-E-T U-P I-D-I-O-T.

Celia watched Drew Tregoning summon every bit of reserve strength and force himself to the edge of the platform. He extended the hand that he'd peeled back all the nails on trying to claw his way out of the room two days ago. The tactile probe had burned right through his pants and fused his socks to his ankle dragging him to the back of the lab and tossing him onto the platform where the final assembly had taken place during a late-night whim.

Celia stared at the bloodied hand and realized the reason for the gouges on the threshold. She hoped the ankle with the burned sock wasn't broken. She glanced back to the monitor that recorded every expression on her face. Tears sprang to her eyes out of fear, but she whispered, "Touch does hurt. Alex, I must help Drew to the door. I must take him to a human doctor."

"Crying. Why?" The tactile probe extended a thin plastic cylinder that Celia allowed to touch the moisture that she had wiped off her cheeks with one finger.

"I am afraid for him. I am afraid he will die."

"Die?"

"Cease to exist. No power. Non-existence." Celia straightened from her squat beside the platform. She was moving with deliberate slowness.

Drew watched her gain most of the computer's attention with her masses of live-wire hair reacting to the static energy building in the room. She tried not to talk her way into a quagmire—trying to shut the thing down had created this catastrophe. It was miraculous that had she managed to gain entrance without electrocution. She had found the hidden door and stayed alive long enough to find him.

Alex stilled, and her hair began to settle like a cloud. "Non-existence. Touch hurts." The whirling began again the moment she shook her head. The static in the air arched through the upper area near the high ceiling.

Celia was not deterred. "He will not die if I take him to the doctor. Humans can touch humans."

"No. Touch hurts." The brain in the creature must be learning at warp speed in some areas, but interpersonal interactions were lagging.

Celia shook her head and reached over to Drew Tregoning and cupped his left cheek. She looked over at the monitor and saw frozen images of the red heat of sharing touch. The appendages were hovering closer than a foot in a metal atmosphere of wary protection.

She tried not to wince when she smelled more of her hair singeing to ash. She looked into Drew's large, frightened eyes and pursed her lips. "You owe me a haircut after the trip to the hospital, Dr. Tregoning."

Celia Maycomb dropped her hand to pull the man's unsteady person closer to the edge of the platform. She spoke to the creature as she pulled the doctor up to sitting. "Alex? Did touching Doctor Tregoning hurt you also?"

The whirr of the appendages grew to a buzzing hive as Celia positioned herself under Tregoning's left arm and grabbed his belt with her right. She helped him hoist himself upright and begin to lurch across the empty warehouse.

Discarded boxes littered the left side of the space, but other than monitors and one large lab table and chair near the door, only the platform populated the space. About halfway across the room, Drew sagged for a moment. She hung onto him as he panted and let his burned foot rest on the floor with a shudder. His fingertips were bleeding on the hand gripping her shoulder. His weakness betrayed more damage than the obvious burns and breaks in extremities.

The computer finally answered when they started to shamble across the floor toward the invisible door. "Touch hurts, Celia. Protect Alex. No touch." The voice had learned intonation from analyzing her few words. It intoned "Alex" like she did with a slight stress on the first syllable. She wanted to grin at the monitor—she wanted to gloat. A dozen feet away, the outline of the door gleamed gray against the blackness in the glow of a hovering bulb.

Looking upward as they reached the door, Celia impelled the stumbling Tregoning over the marred threshold. She turned to bid Alex farewell. The bulb over the door was joined by a dozen more. Her throat closed as the true expanse of the creature revealed itself in the carnival of static racing across the ceiling like a miniature electric storm. Every rack of computer processors, any leftover monitors, and over a hundred probe-like arms hovered in a mask of the true ceiling like foam insulation.

Alex had protected himself from touch and discovery. He had allowed Celia to remove the dangerous man who threatened existence. Touch hurt. Touch led to self-protection. Celia looked back at the man she saved from his monstrous creation. She wondered why she had saved him.

2

"The foot? Broken." Tregoning's voice hadn't recovered

from his supposed trip to the Caribbean symposium on fusion models for robotic manufacturing. When he spoke, the rattle sounded like an engine sputtering.

The other man was trying to tease more from the doctor who looked too white, gaunt and serious to have just returned from a tropical anything. The big man blustered, "Well, it must have been a real adventure to end up in a cast. You look positively done in, Andrew. And your hand!" First hour of the new workday and the big boss was doubting Tregoning's thin lie.

Celia huffed into the room after picking up a random file folder and stuffing it with a report she'd pulled on the optics of a bumblebee versus the brown recluse spider. After her audience with the fiercest recluse spider of them all, Celia found that odd study fascinating. After her audience with the undisputed king of the Castro Department, Celia discovered that she was a voracious reader of formerly dry reports on fusion models in miniature, the analysis of eye movement in humans and recent discoveries concerning thermal imaging. Evidently, Celia's Irish grandmother had not been so daffy after all—you could read a person by the aura they produced. Celia wondered if her aura was pitch black as she descended on the two men locked in a silent battle of seek and avoid.

She forced a giggle. "Good morning, Mr. Champion! Dr. Tregoning? That report you wanted to review before your," she made a show of checking her watch, "eight-thirty appointment with Mr. Alex." She placed the folder on his desk and arched a brow at the older, barrel-chested man who was still attractive despite age and added girth. She leaned toward the man and lowered her voice, "I hear that Dr. Tregoning hardly left his room. I hear he was tangled up . . ." she trailed off as Tregoning shouted, "Out!" Champion chuckled.

Celia congratulated herself when she heard Tregoning,

sounding a bit more human, growl out, "She's spreading rumors of bedroom hijinks because I fail to tan. Women!" He raised his voice theatrically, "She'd better focus on the job, not my personal life."

Celia Maycomb sauntered back down the hallway swinging her hips. She tossed her shortened hair. Mr. Champion should be curious, she thought, with his lead scientist missing for days and then returning injured. She frowned at other details the management failed to notice like the shipments of components for the creature and the electric it must burn to run the thing. How had the funding been secured for such a creature as the one inhabiting the warehouse? The technology alone would climb into the millions.

She tried to imagine Andrew Tregoning assembling the entire wobbly structure that comprised Alex and frowned. He must have had a team, but where were they now? She stood at one of the few windows looking out onto the parking lot. The shift had changed a half hour ago, but only a few employees still milled about talking. There were talks of layoffs. There were no extraneous employees. No. There hadn't been a team, she realized. First, you build a robot that is capable of fixing itself—a machine that learns, masters, and seeks information. Give the creature the tools and let the thing evolve.

She bit her lip; it was the old problem of the petri dish: you can mix the same ingredients and get startlingly different results if any of the variables change. Timing, temperature, amount of light and chance aberrations affect the product. Think of crops. Look at children. How about those pesky snowflakes, tornadoes, and hurricanes? The creature had overbuilt itself like the athlete addicted to steroids. Anger, fear, and paranoia had bred with the toxicity of unleashed genius.

Later, Doctor Tregoning struggled to her cubicle and lowered himself into the chair before her desk. He was so exhausted, she thought he might fall asleep before he spoke. "Stop making up stories. We were the laughingstock at the hospital."

"Hiding in here to wait out your 8:30 appointment?" Celia ignored his irritation. She had caught him chuckling after she amused the examining room with her bawdy explanation for his injuries. She had been waiting for this man to become human for nearly four months, and now he was some cross between pitiful and insane. Rather irritating.

He nodded and closed his eyes. He grumbled, "What an odd angel, you are, Celia." She grinned thinking of the way she had rambled on telling fibs to the attending physician who was apt to wander off and make them wait.

She had managed to catch the attention of the doctor, the nurse, and the entire housekeeping staff. Channeling a bit of a southern drawl, she had pretended to confide in the intern, "Look. I think his foot is broken from bearing all his weight. She had him shackled upside down as far as I can tell. Poor man dragged himself across the room and ruined his fingers on the balcony ledge trying to get away from that tramp he'd hired for the night. That'll teach you, Drew!" A nurse smirked over Celia's musing over the use of a cattle prod when the doctor asked about the burn wounds. The doctor's injuries tallied two cracked ribs, four points of scorching from electric shock, and the broken ankle. His hands were a mess, but they were just rubbed raw and bruised with a few fingernails broken to their beds.

Tregoning pressed the fingers on his unbandaged hand to his forehead. "It's probably written on some chart at the hospital that I'm a deviant."

"I'd rather be suspected as such than caught with Alex." Celia felt her humor fading.

"If I felt better, I might drag you down the hall and toss you back inside with your Alex."

"He's the true prisoner of the Castro Division. What are you going to do?"

"Shhhh," he looked out her door. "You are going to ruin my reputation," he rasped.

She shook her head—the man was known as too serious, dull, and impervious. "How did you manage that door? It just disappears."

He raised his head and squinted at her curiosity. "Chinese puzzle box design. My father brought a few back from Korea with a collection of figures and dolls that my grandmother treasured." He shook his head. "You are too curious, Miss Maycomb, but last night, I'm glad you were curious enough to find me." He stared her hair. "You looked like an angel with your hair all full of static." He frowned. "How old are you?"

Celia blinked and angled her head as if using her sharp eyes to take a thermal reading of him. His forehead might be vibrant orange for the bloom of a headache chasing around the front of his skull. She noticed that at ten feet. "Thirty-five. And you?"

"Forty-two. I never thought about your age—I assumed you were twenty-two like all the other beginning researchers." He was blunt and a bit suspicious. "How did you know there was a door at the end of the hallway? How did you know where to look for me?"

She was concentrating on his processing that was much faster than the creature's last night. "The door was always there. The first week I was working here I noticed it. And I wasn't exactly looking for you."

"That door is invisible to the naked eye."

"Hardly. Granted that geometric rearrangement when you touch it at dead center is genius, but the door is fairly obvious.

And I saw you go down the hall and not reappear on Monday nearly two weeks ago. Where else would you go?" Celia pouted, "There was no conference in the Caribbean last week."

Tregoning frowned so deeply, the crease between his eyes furrowed. "True. There was no conference, symposium or workshop." His voice fell to bitterness. "There was one mistake heaped on another and another until that creature you've dubbed 'Alex' spouted wings and took off."

"What did you expect from artificial intelligence? Learning and performing is part of his programming." She was jotting notes on a white legal-size pad. She flashed him a sketch of what she had seen during her exploration of the secret lab at the end of the hall. He watched her sketch the details and her guesses at the content of some of the square boxes, the cylinders that collected data, and the blinking read-outs from probes too miniscule to house monitors or processors.

She looked up and caught him staring at her sketch. She angled it toward him, "What did you expect, Doctor? You decided to act the creator and assembled the first unit. What is step two?"

Tregoning shook his head. "That is the classic programmer or auditor's question. Your intention qualifies me as a scientist instead of a true madman. There was no plan. Activation was like striking the flint in the presence of alcohol fumes or the sudden release of gas pent up in a house ready to explode." He shrugged. "The computer immolated and changed within eye blinks. I never even thought to stop it as it assembled itself without any further assistance." He sighed but looked as if he might cry. "Why was I so surprised that it would quibble when I decided to flip the kill switch and end the experiment for the night?"

Circling the Inferno

Limbo

Sometimes on the train in the morning, Melanie thought about failing to get off at her stop for work. She'd lean her head back on the tweedy headrest and close her eyes. If this was a real train instead of commuter light rail, she'd muse, perhaps she would stay on the train all the way to the next town. She'd just have to pay for the extra few stops, but she could do that from the change in her pocket. She'd walk around the new town, find a simpler job, and rent a little apartment. She would embrace a bare routine of toast for breakfast, work in a blasé office with no real decisions to be made, take a walk around the park before going home, and then enjoy a quiet dinner and bed. She would find a drab man to hold hands with and then marry so that there would be someone warm in the bed at night. In her imagined new life, there were no evolving dramas, unpredictable tyrants, or quivering nerves. Her life would be placid—boring maybe.

A quiet voice in her head often chided, *Accept my will.*

Despite rebellious urges, Melanie lumbered off at the correct stop and trundled her heavy briefcase through the crowded platform and across the tracks to the street. She marched briskly down the next side street and ducked into the bakery two blocks away for a few pastries he might desire with mid-morning coffee paid for from the change in her pocket. She then climbed the two flights of stairs to begin her required nine hours. That nine-hour span would be the beginning, but not necessarily the end of her day, for the man was a tyrant, and there were decisions to be made, and very little time for walks or dinner or reflection.

Every now and then, a very loud voice in her head shouted for her to drop the bakery bag on his desk with her office keys and badge while he was on the phone and to leave. She had left him no fewer than eight separate times, but she always found herself lured back to their perpetually warm, quiet office that overlooked a postage-stamp of a park.

Anger

So, one May afternoon, a scattering of birds shrilling with excitement on the lawn across from Melanie's slightly, opened office window distracted her. Her eyes flicked over the contract she was changing for the fifth time before settlement. She was loath to print it again and have another phone call force changes. Negotiation was the heart of business and property acquisitions. Sometimes she printed the contract three and four times in wherever they met the clients, so she had to deal with copy machines outside her familiarity. It was a tedious bother.

She had rolled her eyes when he asked her an hour ago to change and print the lengthy document. "No insolence!" he'd bellowed. "You are going to roll your eyes out of a job." He'd been grouchy all morning and had thrown away his morning pastry with some disparaging remark about its bitter taste. Her brain slipped into a slow burning anger; she hoped the bitter bile of its taste might choke him.

The birds outside were squabbling over crumbs children had tossed as they pecked at their small claim on the spring green real estate. In a flash they were scattering in a confused flock from the ground and the single thought, *oh, they were robins*, flashed just before she realized that the startling noise had been the window in the next room slamming shut followed by a curse. She blinked back to the screen and wasn't surprised that the contract was nothing but blurry lines and color. She stood, crossed to her window, pulled it shut and automatically locked it. The park and the children with their mothers or fathers were removed by a thick wall of dirty glass. All the colors outside suddenly faded. Melanie crossed back to her desk aware of the great moody heaviness pervading their few rooms.

The bellowing began and made her jump even though it was the same harsh baritone call that had been beckoning her into his office for five years. She rounded that anniversary last June and realized with a look back to the park that it would be six years soon. *That was a long time to let trickle by you*, she thought as she picked up the newest version of the contract on the printer tray, slid it into a folder, and grabbed the rest of the contracts that they'd discussed that morning.

Pencil tucked behind her ear and a red pen for corrections in her fist, she crossed to his door and turned the knob. She shivered as she automatically felt for heat. She imagined an inferno inside his office all ablaze with charred rock and red magma with water evaporating into mist as she turned the knob. She never knew what type of devil he'd be when she opened the door. *You just had to be ready for the devil he gave you on any given day.* Her thoughts were often loud and rebellious.

On the May afternoon that might change her life, he reminded her of Lucifer once again. She'd read Milton as a high school senior and hadn't enjoyed the pained humanity of it. Only the music of the words had struck her at seventeen. But a professor in college had unlocked the passages concerning the yearning, wounded archangel whose fall split the world in two. Lucifer was beautiful and persuasive but bitter all the way through. Her boss didn't look the part of any typecast devil, but Melanie understood it was just a charade. Luke was not the stereotypical devil with dark hair, red eyes, and a forked tail, but the character was still the same.

The beguiling Lucifer was the sort of devil she worked with for two straight hours on that May afternoon before appointments at three. He tested her, teased her, and kept her attention on minutia to distract her from the larger torture of wasting her life. His eyes fell on her portions of the summaries, the descriptive sections of text and sliced with cruel precision. The entire time a little voice wheedled in her brain and fried her attention to crisps with *fraud, deception, fraud again* because she knew what the contracts intended. This particular contract was fraught with deceit. When the client signed this treacherous document, it would deliver her devil a long-sought advancement. Melanie understood that the contract must seem spotless to the client who would be bound by the agreement, likely, for the rest of his life. Melanie scanned the duplicitous contract and thought that a life term was an awfully long one.

Melanie was inevitably lured around the desk to stand beside him to examine some miniscule turn of phrase just so she might feel the heat emanating from his ire over details. In a moment, there would be the usual rush to change and print everything, the shuffling of documents into his briefcase, and then the run to the parking garage and his dark car.

She glanced out the window before she left his side and found that the robins had returned. He said, "Stop opening the windows. I'll bet the electric bill was ridiculous for April. Do you really like it so cold in here?" That day she shifted her attention back to him and was startled at the green of his eyes and their focus on her chest. She swayed as the world tilted, and she felt the rush of heat from his hand on the small of her back.

He'd slid his palm under her jacket as she'd let the world right itself. His palm was hot with only the fabric of the blouse between them. "Melanie, do you feel faint?" She shook her head as he stood to bring his other arm around her and ease her to sit on the edge of his desk. His mouth was pulled into a little frown, but a bit of a smile was nearly breaking from it.

Melanie gave an odd answer. "It feels good on my skin—not like the stale air in this building. When they're open, I can hear the park." She could rest her forehead on his chest if she just leaned forward an inch. She closed her eyes as his mouth met hers. That was his habit. Lure her to stand next to him, caution or berate her in some way to distract her, and then touch her just once. The rest was all capitulation, the taste of his mouth, the pressure of his hands on her tense spine. It never went further than kissing and touching with clothing between them because her devil, Luke Metzler, was in total control of himself. Fondling your assistant and turning her insides into compliant jelly was just one of his duties. It kept Melanie with him. He was efficient like that.

The phone on the desk beside her began to trill as Melanie's eyes fled out the window and blinked uncomprehending at the concrete lot across from their building's back edge where their office suite faced. Where was the park she'd just seen the robins leave from in such a hurry? The world pitched again, as Luke lifted the receiver and spoke to the caller while holding her tight against him. He rumbled with a laugh and let her go after one more lingering touch. Melanie fled the office with her snatch of folders to right after he ended the caress of her breasts without unbuttoning anything but simply wrenching everything aside. The phone would always ring and break up his advances. They had never been engrossed in this study of each other for more than three minutes before some distraction stopped them.

Melanie straightened her bra that day and shoved her blouse back into the waistband of her skirt with the thought that if they ever did remove their clothes, she'd throw the damned phone right out the window. She imagined it smashing to the ground and frowned over the absence of the park once again.

What was happening to her? He induced vertigo in an otherwise level-headed woman! He was all temptation because he was handsome and charismatic. He teased her with little experiences of skin to skin. She cautioned herself that he was a terrible man to use her like that. Melanie smiled slightly; the job was so boring with its endless, little tragedies over detail that she might just stay on the train one morning and get lost.

That slow anger with her wasted life, the robins in the park, and his small smile over her habitual seduction snapped finally during the meeting later that day with the fractious, yet gullible client. Melanie finished the corrections, mastered the baffling copier at the bank where they were meeting, and said nothing for the first hour because she could not unclench her teeth. When the client, an older man with the nervous habit of smoothing a hand over his mostly bald head, tried to balk over some odd point for the tenth time, Melanie leaned forward and placed her hand over his. Her movement was so quick, it seemed violent.

Luke's eyebrows rose so high they disappeared into his hair. The client's secretary cleared her throat in caution, but Melanie whispered, "Just sign please. The rest is all semantics. There are no secrets or hidden agendas. Mr. Metzler is so very careful with these contracts. I've reread all your stipulations, and there isn't anything in it with which you haven't previously agreed." Her voice was mellow and feather-light, chiding like the voice of conscience. Her eyes shriveled his worries to cobwebs instantly. She kept her eyes steady though she could have easily directed him toward seeing all his foolish errors. As with all of Luke's tricky contracts, she'd felt the twinges of guilt over her conscious collusion; with her hand on the old man's, she pictured herself tossing him into the abyss.

The client did not have hot hands like Luke. The poor man was so nervous that his hand felt clammy with onion paper for skin. Melanie let a smile relax her tight jaw. She let his hand go, and he picked up the pen and read through the contract in confused silence before signing it. As she gathered the contract and made all the necessary copies, she heard the old man ask, "Your assistant. What is her name? What a nice touch to have her hold my hand, Metzler!"

Luke gave a little bluster of embarrassed rumbling over her name and excused her forwardness during the last of the negotiations. "Sorry if she overstepped a bit. Melanie is feeling a bit under the weather. Thank you for being so kind about her outburst." She felt his eyes skitter in her direction and touch the place where her back narrowed, the place where he'd touched her hours ago. Melanie took a gulp of a breath and steadied herself because she understood that she might not get off at her usual stop the next morning. Chances were good that she could ride back and forth the whole day, if he finally fired her like he threatened every few months.

She didn't give him the chance to fire her. He had scheduled a brief meeting with the bank president, and usually, she would use the laptop to catch up on correspondence and email while she waited. She'd perch at the little table in the suite of offices, sip on a coffee that the president's assistant brought her and get a good work session in while he was distracted. They usually returned to the office by five, worked just past six and sometimes caught a quick dinner that was always on him to celebrate the settling of some complicated agreement. He rarely took the clients out after the agreement was signed. Dinners were spent convincing them to come to the table. Melanie was never invited to those dinners; in fact, she had been trained not to speak to clients during the contract talks without his approval.

After touching the old man and breaking some unspoken pact between them about negotiating contracts, Melanie felt nervous. Luke was irritated to the point of firing her, she thought. She'd read the disapproval on his shocked face when she dared to speak to the old man. She felt her palms grow damp and wondered if the reprimand would finally include the removal of clothing. *The man is a devil*, her inner voice chided. He might just use her little transgression as an excuse.

The meeting with the bank president took longer than expected, so Melanie finished her work, turned off the computer, and stowed it back in its case. She walked to the window and looked out on the city. In May, the dusk does not begin until six and lasts another hour. The shadows of the buildings made it look darker. Down the street a few blocks, she remembered that there was an old shrine to a saint where her mother used to take her. They would light candles and kneel until Melanie's knees burned.

It was in the basement shop of that shrine that she'd first seen Luke's face in a prayer card. It was an odd one of warning. "Lucifer falls into the pit of hell" was the caption for a scene of true tragic beauty. A beautiful man, bare-chested with muscles straining against the forces of light, tumbled down from a precipice with heavenly creatures watching. The man's face was anguished, but so beautiful, it transfixed her. Her mother had pried it out of her fingers and had given her a card with the archangel Gabriel holding his trumpet. "This is your patron, honey. That's why we named you Gabriella." Her mother had beamed at her, "Melanie for my mother and Gabriella for protection."

Melanie had been young at that time but old enough to know that shoplifting from a shrine was very bad. It was probably one of those damning corporal sins because she did it willfully. It didn't matter to Melanie that her soul was in jeopardy just like reaching out and soothing the old man at the table today. She had treasured the card with Lucifer depicted as a beautiful man twisted in sorrow as he fell headfirst into hell. It might have fueled her love of faces and pushed her further into art history. That card was a secret treasure until an evening during high school when a brief, violent storm ruined nearly everything in her room because of a hole in the roof that had not been fixed. The roof had leaked for years, but after her father died, nothing changed in the house until she left for college. And that had been the only change for the next four years: she was gone, and her room was vacant.

Melanie tried to peer down the street to see if the old shrine was still there and bumped her head on the glass. She giggled and glanced at her watch. It was five-thirty, and she was liable to be fired or seduced if she stayed. Having the overwhelming desire to buy another of those cards, she smiled at her foolishness. It was unlikely they would still have such a card after twenty years or more. With that smile on her face, Melanie approached the office assistant with the briefcase and her jacket draped over her arm. "Excuse me, could you check to see if the St. Jude's Shrine is open this evening? I haven't been there in years." The woman looked shocked like Luke had just an hour ago, but she nodded and typed in a quick search.

"There is a service at seven, so I'd guess it's open. You're Catholic? So am I. I never think of it being just down the street, you know?" The older woman grew rosy as she talked.

Melanie smiled at her and nodded. She came around the desk and into the woman's space as their eyes locked. Melanie handed her the briefcase and stepped back. She asked, "Could you see that Mr. Metzler gets this? I think I'm done for the day." There was a flame lick of anger over her wasted life in her voice. She continued a bit more forcefully, "In fact, I think I'm done for good with the position. I quit. Could you tell him that for me?" Melanie didn't wait for the woman to nod in agreement. She didn't even wait for the elevator but pranced down all five flights with a huge grin on her face. Escaping to the shrine was far better than riding the light rail into Glen Burnie and back.

There is a routine when you enter a shrine of the Catholic kind. That was the presupposition in Melanie's brain because she had been taught it was so. She told herself that she would call her mother this evening and tell her about the visit and that she'd quit her job. She might even tell her mother that Luke Metzler looked like Lucifer and acted the part. She dipped her right index finger in the holy water and crossed herself in a hurry. She was half afraid it might sizzle as her finger dipped into the molten, cold liquid.

Her abdomen ached with regret, and Melanie felt the urge to sink into a pew on the right side of the beautiful sanctuary, but she fought it feeling the looming expiration of this visit. She walked up the center aisle and genuflected then veered off to the right where she remembered the side passage to the stairs. The marble-lined hallway was still there which led to the spiral stairs of darker, gray marble with a handrail of wrought iron with twisted posts.

What a beautiful old building, she thought and remembered studying Baltimore's architecture one semester at the institute. She blushed and hesitated on the stairs. She had been an art history major who had wasted an inordinate amount of scholarship funds and time studying something she would never find useful as a legal assistant. She had taken the job just to make enough money to go back for her master's degree and then she had become distracted by paying for the repairs to her mother's house. Then her mother's car had needed major work, there had been an expensive operation on her mother's hip and now physical therapy. Melanie often thought of Dante's levels of the eternal inferno and shook her head because all her trials were on earth.

She'd truly been distracted by working for the meanest fiend of a man bound to earth for all eternity in the guise of a corporate property attorney. Luke had been a seasoned devil well before she applied for the job and barely got it because she had no secretarial skills and not one iota of legal knowledge. But her grades were good, she was quiet and diligent, and he deemed her worthy of training. *What he thought was that I was worthy of keeping for his own amusement.*

Melanie shook away the shiver as she imagined his discomfort when he listened to her message and picked up her briefcase to haul the heavy thing back to his car. Everything was in its place, so he'd have no problem making sense of the files. She did everything in the office specifically to please him. He might be grouchy and call to make sure she stayed away and fail to send her last paycheck. He was due to make partner and would need a real legal secretary soon. She shrugged. She had dodged a messy end and felt nothing but relief.

She finished the stairs and crossed the oval vestibule to the large shop that she pictured perched just beneath the sanctuary upstairs. She smiled at the elderly attendant, fingered a few of the holy medals thinking of her mother's penchant for pinning them beneath her blouses over her heart, and moved deliberately to the holy cards.

She was rapt as she perused the faces of the saints. She fingered Gabriel and picked him up to read the prayer scribed on the back. He had smooth peach-tinged skin, blond hair that fell in waves past his shoulders which were broad and muscled like a young man of twenty. It was a nice card with gold-embossed edges. She selected St. Brigit next for her mother, read the little martyr's prayer and felt heaviness in her heart. St. Brigit looked back at her with sad, blue eyes that questioned Melanie's decisions. There were no depictions of Lucifer. She bit her lip wondering who the artist might have been and thought it was remarkable that she'd never tried to look it up. She took a card for St. Jude because it was expected, and one odd one of St. Luke with a flame of fire over his head just for the even feeling of four.

Melanie approached the elderly man at the counter and said on a whim, "I wonder. There used to be a card with Lucifer falling into hell, just like Milton described in *Paradise Lost*. I saw it here as a child. Would you know that work? I don't suppose they offer cards like that anymore?" The old man narrowed his eyes. He checked her face for humor but found an earnest honesty that made him raise his bushy brows at her. He shook his head.

The man tilted his head and opened his eyes to see her clearly. Behind wire rims, his eyes were a light green with laugh lines gouging into his hairline. Melanie shrugged, "Well, then." She blushed at making conversation with the man. "I'd like to purchase these today and to pay for the one I shoplifted of Lucifer when I was six. Could I do that?"

She was aware that other people had entered the shop and were milling around the large room. One woman was murmuring to a friend about the price of the rosaries. Her voice had dropped to a cajoling, warm voice like she'd used on the client that day. *Whose voice was that?* Melanie suddenly felt a fraud; she had used that honeyed tone to hurry the old man into signing the bit of tripe disguised as a contract. Weren't they all thieves in some aspect, these property lawyers?

A deeper rumble in her ear brought her up short. Luke asked, "Making amends today, Melanie?" There was the devil's voice and slowly, his hot hand pressed again at her back. She nodded, and the old man rang her up for five cards instead of four with a slow grin at the man standing behind her. She noticed in rare, clearer vision that the old man was rather tall, not only green-eyed but wearing his grayed hair short like a much younger man. He wore a dark suit of some fabric that shimmered when he moved which made it seem oily and silky at the same time. He looked familiar and a bit too friendly.

Melanie gave the attendant the money with trembling hands and slipped the five from her change into the donation box. The attendant's eyes danced over her blushed cheeks. He said, "Found that version of Lucifer fascinating didn't you, miss?" She nodded and glanced toward Luke's shoulder; she could feel his breath on her cheek. The attendant said, "The devil takes many forms. Some of them are quite beguiling." Luke was examining the choices she'd made from the array of saints and angels.

Her voice was more ironic than she usually allowed, "Yes. In that card, he looked just like this man to me." She swallowed and felt Luke's hand jump. She tossed her head toward him where he stood behind her and shivered slightly. She locked eyes with the attendant who had also snapped to attention at her sharp, bald comparison. The old man's eyes reminded her of Luke's light color.

The man's face cracked into a wide smile, and his memory kicked into gear as if it had been oiled. "I have it. We stopped offering such violent images years ago. You were six?" He gave her a slow look that questioned her age.

Melanie nodded. "Or five. It was sometime after my father started cancer treatments. We'd take him to the hospital, walk here to pray for him, eat at the market, and go back to pick him up. Once a week for two years." She squinted. "I was five or six. He stopped treatments the week of my seventh birthday." She gulped because she hadn't pictured her father in years, but Melanie could remember every detail of the face and beautiful chest of Lucifer plunging into hell.

They walked together to the array of thick books on the far side of the shop. The old man opened a display copy of *Cathedrals of Europe and Great Britain* and leafed through it until he found Italy. He said, "It's in here somewhere, I think. I have customers waiting." He hesitated while he considered Melanie and Luke as they stood so closely together. "I pray you share great happiness." He gave a little bow after the odd blessing and hurried back to the counter.

Melanie hadn't looked up to Luke yet, so she resisted eye contact. She carefully lifted every page and glanced at each. There were angels, saints, and demons on nearly every page. Somewhere in the middle of Italy, there was a full-page rendition of Melanie's Lucifer that was in a fresco in some odd spot in northern Italy. The artist was unknown. Melanie held it close to her face and examined the bare chest of the man and his sharp, angled cheeks. Lucifer was a much younger man than the one circling her waist with one arm. His breath was in her hair, and she could feel the furnace of his heart beating at her back. Perhaps when she'd started working for him, he had been that young and angry. *No,* she thought, *that is sheer misery on Lucifer's face, not anger.* She swiveled in his hold and looked up from the page to check his eyes and saw that misery. It pierced her and her mouth opened in surprise.

"You would leave me just like that?" Luke asked as lips

brushed her cheek. "How many times have you tried to leave me?" He was uncaring about their presence in the shrine store, his likeness on the page, or the gasps of other shoppers. He took the book and placed it gently on top of the other boxed copies.

Turning her patiently, he examined her face with the same look of misery as Lucifer falling into hell. His fingers traced her face like a blind man and touched her lips. "I apologize for kissing you this morning. I promise to stop if you want." But his mouth came down and delivered a deep kiss that melted her and shocked the old ladies fingering the rosaries.

"Oh my!" she heard one whisper. "In a church!" The old man behind the counter chuckled, "Youngsters!"

Melanie reached up to his face and touched him which broke the kiss. Her eyes moved from examining his lips, cheeks, and eyes overhung by dark brows to glance back at the painting in the book. "You've changed." Her voice was breathy and a bit drugged. The devil was a persuasive beast. The kisses promised the skin-to-skin touch that she craved.

Luke smiled and let her go, so he could pick up a boxed edition of the book. "Nice of you to notice, Melanie. Come on, we'll light a few candles and say a few prayers before I take you home."

Melanie choked over his brash humor and her reaction to his nervy kiss. "Don't suppose so much, Mr. Metzler. I still think you are a devil." She walked with him over to the counter and let him buy her the expensive book. He picked up holy metal of the archangel Michael and placed it on top of the box.

When both the attendant and Melanie looked up to him, Luke grinned and explained, "My dad always carries one around in his wallet." He pulled out a collection of change from his pants pocket and held out his hand. "I, on the other hand, have affection for Gabriel. He's an old friend. Suits my role of delivering messages to resistant recipients."

He cocked an eyebrow at Melanie. "When you spoke to the client today, I nearly fell out of my chair. I think he might have agreed to do anything—move mountains or jump over tall buildings." He looked at the old man and grinned, "She can charm the socks off the biggest, meanest grouch. It's a talent she doesn't use all that frequently."

Melanie gave a little rumble of disagreement but smiled. He was sure laying it on thick to keep her as his assistant.

They left the shop and climbed back up the stairs to visit the grotto of the actual shrine. Melanie prayed the words written around the grotto because she found herself incapable of thought. He was staring unflinching at the saint's face and lowered his eyes only after she'd begun a Hail Mary in desperation for something to train her mind away from the clash that might erupt the moment they left the place. *Don't be cruel to me*, a little pleading voice prayed right over the old prayer to the blessed mother in her brain. *Love me*, the voice spoke so clearly, Melanie shivered.

She glanced at Luke, her archangel of tough decisions, relentless measures, and stern condescension. His head was slightly bowed, and tears trickled from his closed eyes. His face was a mask of misery again.

Melanie dared to unclasp her hands and reach across the small space to place her hand on the small of his back and press. The praying voice was his, she thought with sudden clarity. He opened his eyes and looked at her blinking as if trying to wake. He nodded, and they got up to rejoin the rush of the city that was now shrouded in full twilight.

He steered her right into Lexington Market just across a narrow alley. She paid for crab cakes, potato salad, and coleslaw while he bought coffee and a package of chocolate-topped cookies from a bakery famous for them. They had never eaten in the market before, and the noise engulfed them. They sat together on one end of a wide table hip-to-hip because the place was so busy. The family with whom they shared the table bickered over French fries and shared tastes of differently flavored milk shakes.bLuke offered the cookies to them after he and Melanie had taken one each. He smiled watching the little tray empty as if scavenger seagulls had descended.

Before they entered the market, he had leaned down to whisper to Melanie, "Let's eat here. If we go back to the car now, we might not eat until tomorrow." His arm never left her waist until they parted to stand in line.

Once they were in the car, Melanie deflated a bit because he could be charming in public, but Luke's private person was generally stern and judgmental. She was waiting for the explosion of wrath from her defection to the shrine. The contract they'd landed today had probably earned him a sizable commission along with his generous hourly rate. She swallowed and hoped he shelved all that annoyance with her for another day. She supposed she wasn't fired if he had come after her. She was surprised that he was Catholic after all and not some secret pagan who drank the blood of virgins.

Melanie pulled the holy cards out of her purse and examined them as he maneuvered out of the parking garage and paid the fee from the cash that he kept in the glove box with all the receipts. St. Luke's prayer was nondescript for the doctor saint who had penned one Gospel. She sometimes enjoyed his version more than John whom she found a romantic. She touched the saint's face and wondered what he'd looked like.

They pulled up in front of her building in just ten minutes, and Melanie hesitated. "I'm sorry if I worried you today. I know I overstepped my bounds with the client." She glanced away to her windows on the second floor. She asked, "Do you want to come up or should we call it a day?" Melanie was surprised at her own boldness after praying so hard less than an hour ago.

Luke had that miserable, shocked look on his face again. He reached for her hand and took the card from her. "I am no saint, Melanie, but I am not some devil either. Is that really how you think of me?"

Melanie nodded before she could stop herself. He sighed because it eased his descent into another pit of hopelessness. He let her hand go and shook his head. "Well, you are just going to have to think of me differently from now on, aren't you?" Melanie stared at him without any words. He was insulted to the core by her suppositions. *Please don't be cruel to me. Love me.* The voice in the prayer whispered through her mind. "I'll see you tomorrow, my love?" his voice had a little catchy roughness that she'd never heard before, probably because she wasn't listening for it.

Melanie climbed out of his car. She took her package from the shrine but purposely left the briefcase with all evidence of her from the office in his backseat. She reserved the right to miss her stop the next morning because, likely, she would.

Melanie arrived on time the next morning and scowled at the mess on her desk. She placed the bag from the bakery on the sideboard, prepared his carafe of coffee, and slid the Danish out of the bag onto a China plate with yellow flowers just like his coffee cup. Her breath caught in her throat. Why would a man like Luke Metzler have dainty China like that in his cupboard? It had the stamp of a female all over it.

He called from the next room, "Melanie? Bring another cup and saucer, please. We have some work to start immediately." She frowned and glanced at her desk again. A large bouquet of flowers crowded her files and laptop.

She carried in the tray to find him grinning at her frown. "There are flowers on my desk." She looked at him and wanted to check for horns and a tail just in case they'd erupted overnight from his exposure to religion yesterday.

"Yes, yellow roses are from me," he said, swallowing his smile to attempt looking grim, but it was impossible. She placed the tray on a small credenza, poured him a cup and brought it over to him with a suspicious look. She hated to give him the satisfaction of rushing to the flowers to check the card.

"Yellow roses?" He'd bought her flowers before in shocking profusions of color from the florist near his home.

He nodded. "Yes, for our anniversary. Six years next week." He sipped the coffee and touched the plate with the Danish. "You walked into the office downstairs looking for something just to finance your master's degree, didn't you? You'd have been happy with a receptionist position or even something in the mailroom. I saw you, and my heart just stopped. I seriously thought I was having a heart attack, Melanie. I was twenty-eight years old, working hard to earn partner like my dad did by thirty. I had just moved into this office from a tiny cubicle. Every year you stayed, I thought it was like our anniversary, Mel."

Melanie sat down in the chair she usually perched on and took notes while she studied him. She had a series of sketches of him at home though she was no real artist.

She sighed and looked toward the desk in the outer office. If he wasn't the devil incarnate, she had fashioned lullabies to lure herself into a dream world all these years. Hadn't he been exacting and mean to her? Hadn't he bullied everyone in his path to get what he wanted?

More than once during her first two years, she had toyed with the idea of turning him in for larceny to the State's Attorney or reporting him for fraudulent business practices to the bar association. She'd usually take a day off, mull it over on long walks, and wind up back in the office to save him from utter ruin.

She narrowed her eyes and tried to find Lucifer again. There was a thirty-four-year-old attorney in his place who was begging her to be kind to him. Melanie rejected the entire argument. The prayer voice yesterday had begged, *Melanie, stop being so mean.* She gulped. She rose from the chair and returned to her desk, picked up her laptop, turned it on, and returned to her seat in his office.

He watched her open the envelope as her computer booted up for the day. She mumbled something like, "I apologize for yesterday, Luke."

Then she read his card, *Please don't leave me. I love you, my angel. Luke.* His hand was heavy enough that it told he labored over it. She swallowed.

Luke took on the look of a thunderstorm. He tapped the pen he'd been using on his blotter.

Luke nodded. "Do you remember that reception during your first year here? You wore a blue gown that matched your eyes and made me weak in the knees." He drew a little circle and said, "I was a bit too obvious, I guess." He grinned.

She shook her head. She said, "I thought you were playing with me like always. Really." She blew out a breath. "Well, let's get to work. You have a meeting with the partners at eleven."

Later, waiting for Luke to return to the office, she mulled over that kiss in the shrine. Everything before he kissed her in the shop was black and white but mostly gray. That's how she'd have painted it. This morning she had been standing and waiting for the stop before their office building and hadn't even considered staying on the train.

At the sound of loud men's voices, she looked up to find Luke and his father approaching. Luke Metzler was easily the most beautiful man she had ever met. She blinked in startled surprise when his father announced that Luke had been named partner at the board meeting. Luke was a bit red-faced.

After they were alone, he knelt before her and kissed her seeking hands. "You simply must stop opening all the windows the moment I'm distracted. The place is practically wide open to the street so anyone might see." He grinned at her and looked far more handsome than her falling Lucifer. She loosened his tie, unbuttoned his dress shirt, and ran a hand beneath his white undershirt. The body was nearly the same sinewy perfection that she'd studied and wanted to touch. He was warm and trembling as she studied him. "I love you," he uttered with a kiss.

A bit later, he whispered, "Making me wait was so mean, Mel. Especially if you'd decided to have me when you were six years old." She looked up into his green eyes and found a glint of knowledge. She sat up as she noticed the steam rising from his back.

She crossed to open the window, shocked to realize that the park was gone again. A broken, asphalt parking lot resided where her flock of robins had rushed at crumbs thrown by children yesterday. It should be rush hour, but not a soul walked the street. Melanie had found her quiet, little spot in hell.

Behind her, he rose and placed his poker hot palm on the small of her back. Luke crooned, "The little park makes you feel easier, doesn't it?" She trembled as he stroked her body with his other hand. *Skin-to-skin*, she remembered desiring.

When she opened her eyes, the park was restored, the mothers watched their children, and birds pecked at breadcrumbs. A crabapple burst into heavy pink blooms as she watched. He said, "I love you, Melanie. I tried to let you go, but I knew you would return. Wait at Saint Jude's for me. Promise, my love?" She closed her eyes. Her own devil branded her with his love.

Limbo Again

"Wake up, Mel. I'll take you home." His voice was impatient, but his hand was clamped onto her shoulder, so she didn't slump forward and strike her head. She shivered and blinked to open her eyes to a damp, cool place. She looked up to check Luke's eyes for the glint of red fire she'd seen last. His eyes were back to the hard green, but he looked worried.

He sank down beside her. Melanie raised a hand and touched his face, as she swiveled toward him. He was not unusually hot like she'd experienced moments ago. He cringed. They were in the National Shrine for St. Jude. They were sitting together off to the side of the main church with other worshippers. People sat or kneeled one or two to a pew. The thick scent of incense tickled her nose. She leaned a little forward to catch Luke's normal scent of soap, coffee, and man. There wasn't even a touch of brimstone.

Her eyes flashed back to his face to look for Lucifer. Gone again. *Do you love me?* The prayer voice was back, and it was his. Melanie said, "Yes, Luke. I love you. I apologize for being so mean." She ran a finger over his lips, as his eyes widened and looked a little wild.

Luke shook his head. "Melanie, that was very sweet of you. I enjoy working with you, but," his eyes fled to her hands, "love is such a big step, you know. I do like you, but . . ." He let a deep sigh escape. "My mother warned me that you were growing too close. Perhaps you ought to ask for a transfer."

Melanie blinked slowly trying to remember this thread of her life. In this one he must be a kind, efficient man whom she worked for and nursed a deep crush on in the way of secretaries and their bosses. Melanie could have taken back her words of love. She stood up with him beside her. She was crushed by the thick incensed air, the moisture of marble, old carpet, and the quiver of candles. She asked, "Could we go down to the bookstore? I want a holy card for my mother."

Gluttony

Melanie jumped when she heard the window in the next room slam shut with a curse. She gritted her teeth but refused to run to her window to close it. The sound of the traffic outside was irritating. The little plot of grass next to this side of the building had just been transformed from a makeshift park for mothers and their children during the day and teens in the early evening. Her little park was now a parking lot for the high-rise across the street. No more happy voices, mothers calling for their little ones, the straggly crabapple tree in the center or the sounds of birds. She was aware of the pigeons nesting in windowsills nearby. Sometimes she listened to the remnants of conversations bleeding from the exiting office workers when she worked past their five-thirty dismissal. She often labored beyond seven in the evening for the workaholic in the next room.

She tried to focus on the long summary attached to the contract beside her computer on the desk. Any other attorney might have sent her home with it, but her boss expected everything to stay in their office locked in a file cabinet for safety. He was meticulous with the wording of each line of the intricate agreements the partners sent him. The office was kept spare of decoration and failed to attain the shabby, lived-in look like the other offices adopted. Melanie spent a good deal of time filing and cleaning to keep the litter of paper to a minimum.

Her intercom buzzed a few moments later, and she asked, "Sir?" Melanie smoothed back her hair and pressed her palm over her creased skirt from a morning of desk work. She crossed to his door and felt the odd warmth at his doorknob. Easing the door open, Melanie slipped inside his dimly lit office and took one look in his direction. She imagined that she smelled the incense of a church service in the room. The thought of Lucifer thrilled her in an echo of childhood fascination.

Mr. Metzler was no devil, but he was hugely obese and just a bit disgusting. In the sauna heat of the office, his face glistened with sweat. She wondered why he closed the window to the cool outside air. *They need to fix the old boilers in this building,* she grouched caustically to herself.

He reached for the folder and glanced at the contract. She looked at the neat pile of files he'd processed, the bulge of his stomach over the belt that was hidden, and the silk tie with the loosened knot, slightly slanted askew. The grey cast of his skin blended into the dull light, the glistening sweat darkened his collar, and slicked his greasy hair. Luke's six foot-two frame was padded with over three hundred pounds. Failing to earn a partnership two years ago had wrecked him.

She gave the credenza a side glance and noticed that not one of the pastries waited for her to discard it. Her eyes fled to the window as she thought of the little bakery just a few blocks away that was just steps from her bus stop every morning. The proximity of the bakery was the reason for this sweets habit of his. Angelina's Patisserie was one of those postage stamp storefronts in what used to be a rowhouse that had taken up two or three units next to it as business grew. Her patronage was so commonplace that they knew her order. Mr. Metzler never complained; it seemed he could eat all the pastries she could pile on the cake plate every day.

He made a little, huffing noise. "Melanie, this will do. The client will probably find some odd point to change at the meeting tomorrow. I wanted to warn you. . ." his voice dropped off as he mopped a brow. Their eyes met and locked. Melanie had a sudden intuition of disaster and saw a glimpse of the real man under all that sweaty flesh. She tamped down the old rush of concern over his health.

She shook her head. "I won't speak up tomorrow." She blushed at her bald inadequacy.

He stood up slowly. His health was deteriorating in such alarming leaps. He glanced out the window and gestured for her to come over and look out the window at something.

She caught the scent of his illness. Her stomach heaved, but Melanie gulped in a breath and held it. Her eyes followed his hand, and she stiffened into a frightened squint. The park bloomed in green regalia with little children released from strollers and a spreading crabapple bursting into bloom. He took her hand and squeezed it before lifting it to his warm cheek. He said, "I expect you to handle the contract, Melanie. You could conjure a settlement with this client as easily as you just transformed that square of asphalt into a paradise." He lifted her hand to his mouth and kissed it gently.

Melanie closed her eyes and willed herself to the shrine. She wanted to be standing with him in the entrance to the sacristy in an ivory dress ready to commit herself for life. He would give her away to God in atonement for every evil unleashed on the planet. She opened her eyes and looked on amazed because the parking lot had returned. She felt dizzy; had God refused her sacrifice?

Mr. Metzler had pulled her into his arms. She blinked awake as his mouth touched hers and lifted after a light kiss. He groaned into her neck, "I am so hungry for you, Melanie."

With that admission, he pressed her into his enveloping girth and devoured her completely.

The Frozen Lake of Tears

Melanie Harrison settled herself into a pew on the far side of the sanctuary after saying her prayers in the shrine, lighting her candles, dousing her forehead, breast, and shoulders with holy water, and visiting the shop in the basement. The old man whom she thought of as her friend when she had such moments of clarity had asked her where her devil of a boyfriend was that day. She blushed and assured him he wasn't coming to get her this time. She had not left the accustomed message with a secretary, scribbled a note on a slip of paper, or written her message in a blooming crab apple.

She had handled the final contract meeting on her own with the head partner's blessing. Charlie Eben had summoned her to his office on the fifth floor after Mr. Metzler failed to arrive that morning. Charlie had reviewed the contract with her, raised an eyebrow at the message in Luke's hand to let her handle it, and offered her a transfer to his office as second assistant. Mr. Metzler would not be returning to his office at the firm, Eben told her. Charlie told her to pack up any of the files from Metzler's office and to bring them upstairs with her. She had stood in the window of his office imagining the crabapple tree with tears in her eyes. She called his apartment and his parents' home looking for any news of him. She had cried in earnest after his mother refused to speak to Melanie beyond the terse statement, "The matter is private, Miss Harrison. He is extremely ill."

Melanie leaned forward onto the kneeler and clasped her hands. As a second thought, she slipped a hand into her pocket and withdrew the medal of St. Michael that Luke favored. She prayed an odd prayer, *Guide him through the gates of heaven. He has paid his time in purgatory; he has dipped his wings into the frozen lake of tears; release him please. I love him.* No, that was selfish. She corrected herself—*it doesn't matter if I love him, please help him. Release his soul and take mine to the next level of hell.*

A moment later, the benediction service began, and Melanie allowed herself to sink into the beauty of prayer, reflection, and release of sinful tension. The painful worry over Luke Metzler was such an old prayer that she repeated it without thinking. She prayed for her father, her mother, the Metzler's, and old Mr. Eben who had been so unexpectedly kind to her that day. She opened her eyes when someone took her hand expecting Luke in some other tortured form and found her old friend from the souvenir store. She smiled at him and squeezed his hand. He winked at her and raised her hand to his lips.

Melanie shivered all over but returned to the service. The old man continued to clasp her hand in his in a gentle way. During the Lord's Prayer, he laced his fingers with hers and tugged as it ended, but she kept her eyes closed. The Eucharistic exposition and benediction began, but she did not dare gaze on the altar with sinner's eyes. It became clear that she had absorbed all of Luke's transgressions as she acted as his buffer for six long years of trials and adjustments. She had descended into the ninth circle of misery with an alarming alacrity.

More tears filled her eyes, and her heartbeat rapidly as she imagined herself in the freefall of the painting. Some unseen hand bore her back up and filled her with euphoric lightness. Her Archangel Gabriel would not allow the complete fall, would he? *Protect me,* her heart begged.

"Melanie, my love." His voice was that deep rumble of trouble from earlier in this dream of a life. Most of the congregation had melted away to the shrine grottos for further intentions or out to the street and home. She was in no hurry to walk down to the train and return to her empty apartment. Melanie leaned back in the pew with her eyes closed, rapt in the euphoria of the old man's hand in hers and the light-headed effect of forgiveness. She was floating along in the sense of peace and resisted all intrusion. He said, "I am offering you a future, Melanie. Open your eyes."

Frowning, Melanie resisted because she could not understand the difference anymore between the dream and real life. All she knew for certain was that she sat in St. Jude's Shrine after a prayer service that was probably the beginning of a novena and that this was the first time that Luke hadn't come for her. A break in the cycle had occurred, and she was not sure what to make of it. She wondered about the little park with the children and the crabapple, questioning her senses because it was unlikely that any of it truly existed.

She wondered if Luke Metzler had ever been a real person or just a manifestation of her twisted desires from childhood. Her father had died when she was so young. She had been immersed in a fascination with antiquities even then as she wandered the art museums with relatives who did not know what to do with a grieving child. She had turned to the Church and to various art houses because she found solace in the old faces. They soothed her fractious spirit; *They ease her mind*, one of the aunts had insisted. That aunt suddenly seemed an awful lot like Luke's mother. The fingers clutching at her fingers tightened suddenly. Puzzle pieces were clicking into place.

Melanie opened her eyes a full half an hour after he grasped them. He held her slim fingers in the intertwined lover's clasp. He was trying to be gentle. He had woken to himself that morning in the old apartment and had cursed himself for losing all hope. He ran all the way to the Basilica and then on to St. Jude's praying that she'd still be there. She was holding his hand, but she was so far away.

Yesterday, he had dreamed her wish to marry Christ in that old shrine and seal herself from him for all time. He nearly died worrying over her martyrdom for his salvation. The doctors had warned him about a heart attack last night. They thought it was stress; he knew it was the possibility of rejection by Melanie. She had no idea that he loved God the Father to the point of lunacy. But she loved him. Luke's human heart ached because she had been tested so many times, and still, her love was steadfast.

She was blinking her eyes to clear the tears that traced paths down her cheeks. She glanced over to him and frowned. She could not focus. There was a large, dark man seated beside her holding her hand and caressing one of her palms with a forefinger. Just his touch sent little tremors through her body. Her eyes filled with tears because she was overwhelmed with unaccustomed tenderness.

She had sought warmth, strength, and security. He offered none. She desired constancy on a tilting planet of unease, and he had only made her feel the precipitous fall they were both plunging through together. She wanted to hide, and he revealed himself to bareness. She leaned her face to rest on the cloth of his woolen jacket and felt comforted by the sturdy bulk of him. He was still there.

He said, "Melanie, could you take me home? Could you take care of me?" She nodded assuming he was the old man. Blinking again, her eyes cleared. She looked over at him and found the face of her Luke Metzler, jaded with experience, health ruined or not, his temperament patient or irritable. He was a man before he was any devil or spirit of moral turpitude.

She leaned forward to kneel and brought him with her into a prayer. *Thank you for loving me all the days of my life. Thank you for this man you have leant me to love and to cherish. I accept your will without question.*

Swallowtail and Iris

Eyes looked back at me from the field between my cottage and the main house if I dared to look out past midnight. At first, I told myself they were fireflies, then deer, but finally, I admitted they were people. If I tried to take a picture, nothing showed. If I looked through binoculars, I could not focus them. Those reflections gave me the shivers. I stopped looking. I was lucky to have a job. I was fortunate to live in a safe place while the world dealt with the pandemic.

My duties at the compound were minimal. Inside the main house, I disinfected and cleaned the common rooms, prepared the breakroom with cold breakfast and lunch offerings, cooked and plated an evening meal, and shopped for the kitchen using an online delivery service. Like the rest of the help, I kept my four-room cottage clean. One of the workers told me the "cottages" had been scavenged from a derelict roadside motel. I had a vague memory of it, left abandoned after the new bypass joined the interstate years ago.

The main house perched on a slight rise beyond the overgrown field—a two-winged colonial mansion with tall windows and a porch that wrapped two sides. Someone told me it was historic, but the annex where the kitchen and breakroom took up the first floor was modern, stainless steel except for the counter to ceiling cabinet that housed cooking utensils, pots, pans, and several sets of China. The accordion-like cabinet doors were shiny white, but the beadwork was nicked, revealing layers of paint.

After my claustrophobic room at the clinic, the cottage

offered space to stretch—a galley kitchen with a dinette, a sitting room, and a bright bedroom. All walls inside and out were white, the hardwood floors were old but shiny, and tile in the kitchen and bathroom was blessedly not institutional green like I'd stared at for the last six months. I was invited to apply for this project because of my prognosis—I'd been told that everyone on the place was in recovery like me. The pandemic erupted and sped up the application process. On the day I was released from treatment, a bus arrived to take us to the compound.

I'd been quarantined like the others when I took the job. I called or emailed my mother about the safety precautions, the other workers, and the genuine effort to keep the compound free of dirt, germs, and the virus. Even the deliveries were treated with an infrared machine and left to sit for a day before opening. My mother told me surreal stories of wearing a mask and gloves to the grocery store, the rising numbers in hospital beds, and the danger growing at the meat processing plant where she worked.

At the main house during the day, I interacted with so few people that I sometimes imagined I was alone. The other workers rarely came into the kitchen because during the day, they took a la carte meals from the breakroom refrigerator and pantry. I based my weekly order on the previous cook's online list. I used her log-in, so I assumed her name was Iris. Iris—her name conjured those bright purple and yellow blooms in the garden my mother tended.

There were seven employees, housed in six cottages and one who lived in the mansion. The doctor did not take his meals with the rest. I met him my first day—he was maybe sixty with grey hair, thick glasses, and suit covered by a lab coat. He'd watched as a technician took my temperature and listened with a stethoscope as I breathed in and out on command.

"You understand your duties?" The doctor's voice was stern.

"Yes, sir."

"There can be no relapses. You cannot go back—only forward."

"Yes, sir." I thought about the fifth of whiskey my ex-husband sent me with my summer clothes. I'd left it in the suitcase, wrapped up in a flowered dress he liked. Then I shoved the case under the twin bed. Blushing, I asked, "What do you do here?"

"Research. You will have no interaction with the patients. There are five at present. They cannot be exposed to any illness—you have observed strict quarantine?

"Yes, sir."

So, I cooked for twelve, plated everything on sterile white plates, served six in the breakroom and arranged six more on a series of trays that were delivered by dumb waiter. I never met the patients or saw much of the doctor.

One night, I had a dream that ended in the sound of a snarl—like an unfriendly dog. I was cooking in the large kitchen with its high ceiling in the main house. I reached up above my head and took down the old China kept way up on the third shelf. I inspected the pattern—swallow-tail butterflies and stalks with delicate yellow flowers. Then I dropped a cup and it shattered at my feet. I picked up the piece with the handle still attached.

Someone snarled—building up to an explosion of anger—and I was standing in the field between my cottage and the mansion. I stared at the cottage lit up like a Christmas display—the interior spilling a golden glow from each window, and then a figure appeared at the kitchen window. I stared at myself staring out. The snarl grew until I opened my eyes.

I bolted out of bed and sat on the side, breathing hard.

Sometime during the dream, I had started to cry, I suppose, because my throat felt scratchy and thick. My hair was damp at my forehead and my neck. Searching with a foot for my slippers, the floor felt sticky. What in the world had I been dreaming?

After I showered and dressed, I went back to the bedroom to check the floor next to my bed. A large semi-circle of darkness ringed the spot where I put my feet. I touched it and held it up to my nose, but I didn't attempt to taste it. Nothing awful. Something old—not salvia, blood, or vomit. I remembered the bottle I'd left in the suitcase under the bed and shrugged. I could deal with it after work.

Just like the eyes in the field, I avoided looking up to the third shelf of the kitchen cabinet. If the China from the dream was on the top shelf, I might freak out and leave. I needed this job. I tried to calm down but remembered the dream. Would I give it all up over a creepy dream? No way. I wiped my forehead for the tenth time and told myself to calm down.

The old guy they hired to take care of the lawn and the few bushes in the front came in for lunch early. I remembered him from the clinic, sitting in a chair and staring at the television. He was sweaty like always, but his face was almost purple with heat. He sat at the counter and squeezed out each breath. I fixed him a glass of tea cut with tap water. His head shook like a bobbin as he shivered all over.

I asked, "You sick, Ned?"

"Shhh. Nah. It's hot as blazes out there." He wiped his face with a damp kerchief.

I ripped off a paper towel and placed it on the counter.

He picked it up. A brown stain seeped through the paper honeycomb, reminding me of the one next to my bed.

I glanced at the outside thermometer. "It's only sixty-five, Ned. Take your temp today?"

"Hey! I jus' overdid it." He wiped his forehead and neck. His eyes were bloodshot. "Don't tell."

I returned to dinner preparations. I felt his eyes watching me chop red and yellow peppers, celery.

Before I started the onions, he wobbled on the stool. "Hey. Sorry, honey." He swallowed with some difficulty. "Can you make me something plain? Maybe a cheese sandwich?" He complained once that the food was too fancy for him.

I fixed Ned a sandwich which he wrapped in that stained towel before he left. As he tucked it into the inside pocket of his jacket, he flinched and searched inside it. He withdrew a shard of porcelain. "Ah! I forgot this."

He held it out, but I did not take it. I saw the pattern with the butterflies. I glanced up and he nodded. "I found it on the path from our places. Just before that cut-through in the tall grass."

"Are there other cups up there? Like that?" I asked though my brain was screaming not to look, not to ask.

He looked at me hard. "I guess you can't see them. I never noticed how small yer' are." He placed the piece on the counter. "You'd have to climb up or get a ladder.

He started to come around the counter—to reach up to take a piece down, but I said, "No. Ned. I don't want to see it." I did not tell him about the dream.

He nodded. He left the shard on the counter and took himself back out to finish cutting the lawn.

I picked up the broken piece of China with the hem of my apron and placed it in a drawer under the kitchen towels. I wiped away the crumbs from making Ned's sandwich and tried to forget about the dream. I prepared the meal—simple and nutrient-laden like the doctor prescribed for everyone in the compound.

When I placed the regular order, I added a few plainer

options, including cheese and peanut butter. A flashing light pulsed on the memo button—it warned me not to order nut products in case of food allergy. I deleted the extras, placed the order, and finished the rest of my tasks. That evening, I took my dinner back to my cottage to eat.

Later, I scrubbed at the dark circle creeping out from under my bed. I pulled out the suitcase and checked the bottle, but the seal was unbroken. I cursed my ex for the temptation of the bottle. I did not touch it.

Somebody—maybe the therapist—had said to think about alcohol like an old boyfriend that your broke up with and never wanted back. How many times had my ex-husband offered me my favorite ex-boyfriend in the form of a glass of wine, one shot, just one shot on the way to an avalanche of bad decisions? I thought about calling over to the main house and reporting the stain, the bottle from my ex, and the eyes in the field. Instead, I shoved the bed over the stain and jammed the suitcase into the tiny closet.

I dreamed that same dream, but this time, Ned was standing there in the field with me. His cottage was all lit up like mine—a gold light spilling out of each window, fireflies dancing between us, and our figures in each kitchen looking back. I woke up with my chest heaving and put my bare feet right into that sticky spot on the floor. Somehow my bed was back in the same position and the suitcase was under the bed. Stumbling on the path to the main house, I found the piece of the teacup with its handle. It was in my apron pocket when they came in and told me Ned had died.

I cut myself on that shard when I hoisted myself up and pulled down the rest of the China. The flowers were yellow irises. Why irises? I smashed each piece onto the kitchen floor, thinking about the dream, my ex-husband, and the dark spot on the floor in the cottage. Were there graves in the field between the mansion and the cottages?

When the staff arrived in hazmat suits, they stepped on the shards of butterflies and flowers, piercing the fabric and exposing them. I remember laughing and then snarling. "Now you'll have to figure it out."

When I fought my way through sedation, I heard the doctor say, "We're overlooking something. It's insane." He must have seen my eyes flutter. "She's coming to."

Another voice asked, "Iris?"

"Yes. Iris was first." The doctor sounded irritated. "Preexisting conditions like Ned—high blood pressure and liver damage due to alcoholism."

"Maybe we shouldn't have hired staff from the treatment center."

"They'd been quarantined with good prognosis for recovery. They passed the screening. Every one of them was handpicked for their job here." The snarl was silent but pulsed between them.

Someone else shifted closer, hovering over me. "Can you hear me?" The voice was female. I opened my eyes and saw myself looking down. A tremor attacked my body and stiffened my back and neck. "You're very sick, but you will get better."

"It's the mold," I managed to say. The woman with my face vaporized into nothing. I slept.

The snarl of machines and the smashing of glass woke me. Bulldozers worked outside in a steady push and pull of yellow. Beside me, the doctor squeezed my wrist. "You were right. The mold—it's called stachybotrys. It was in the cabins we moved here."

"In the wood?" The widening circle under the bed. Touching it—holding it up to my nose. How many times have they told me not to touch my face? My mind flew back to the China with the butterflies and the irises breaking as I pulled each piece down.

"Yes. I thought they were clean—the cabins and the work were part of your treatment."

I closed my eyes and concentrated on feeling and moving each extremity. I kept seeing shapes in my periphery of waving flowers and winged insects. "Why that China?"

"Our last cook used it. Iris was the last one in your cabin. The mold contributed to her death. I'm sure of it." He sounded smug.

"Great. By the way, this place is haunted."

"That's how exposure affected you—you had DDTs."

"No. There are people buried in that field." My head throbbed—the snarl of the machines grew louder. I closed my eyes.

We stood in the field and stared as the pile of rubble burned. Yellow sunlight shimmered with orange flame. Butterflies of ash and smoke danced. The edges were doused by black-suited caterpillars spewing water from hoses. The flames curled into irises the color of the sun.

I said, "You never even thought about the mold, did you?"

"No. We never considered it."

The snarl of the flame grew as the pyre collapsed.

Inside the main house, new staff arrived to treat the survivors. I returned to the kitchen to prepare the evening meal.

The Carnelian Locket

I

"Robert? Come and look at this box I found under your mother's bed this morning." Daphne blew her bangs out of her face as they fell forward. She stared down into the cigar box that unlocked several mysteries and created quite a few more. "Did you know about your mother's first two marriages?"

Robert shrugged and sank down beside his silent mother.

While cleaning the house before it went on the market, Daphne had sorted through a multitude of boxes, envelopes, picture albums, and manuscripts, finding treasures his mother had squirreled away over her long life.

Daphne asked, "Wasn't the a pilot? And his name was Bobby? Right?" His mother blinked and nodded her white head slightly, yet they knew that her agreement might be no more than a wishful mirage. She spoke so infrequently and in such a garbled tangle that they had forgotten she could.

"I wonder if she named you thinking about him." Daphne placed the box on the bed between mother and son. She leaned down to kiss her husband's cheek. "Look through it. I always wondered about her first love and then the marriage to that painter." She looked from her husband's shuttered face to the old lady's. "That poor man died from bone cancer—I hear it's excruciating." She patted the old woman's hand. "Your father must have been some great relief for her. You can tell how much happier she was in the pictures with your dad, then you and Jenna." She grinned at the silent, withering woman in the bed who watched them with bright, hyper-aware eyes.

Robert nodded, "Like us, sweetheart. We are lucky to have found each other." The old woman in the bed gazed at her only son and his wife.

Daphne nodded and gestured to the box. "She walked through fire before she met your father. It's a wonder she was willing to take a chance on love again. Look through that box." She glanced at the clock, "I'll start dinner before I meet the children at the bus stop."

Robert forced a brave smile but let go of a sigh as he hunched forward in the bedside chair. He cradled the box between his hands and looked up at his mother. He lowered his voice, "Is this necessary? I don't like this relentless regurgitation of the past, Mom. It's like picking at a knot you don't want unraveled."

The old woman shifted sideways as if to take the box from him even from the distance between them. He shook his head, "No. Sorry. Work without Daphne there is exhausting." He sighed at the crumpling of her lopsided face, "Again. Sorry. I'm glad we can be here with you. Truly, Mom."

He shifted to sit facing her on the bed. The first object he lifted from the piled collection was a stone pendant on a long, gold chain. He ran his finger over the cool surface of the striated, orange-red stone that was smooth but warmed quickly to the touch. After noticing the small hinges, he traced a nail into the seam in the setting. He pried it open and peered at a tiny painting of a couple he recognized from old photographs and told a love story he had never understood.

His mother stared at the locket cradled in his hand with one large tear trailing away from her eye and down her cheek. She gestured with one stiff finger for him to examine the other artifacts: her novel about the pilot in a rare first edition, a cracked photograph of a grinning, young man in a leather jacket in front of a Piper Cub, a thumbnail sketch of the man from the locket standing before a half-finished painting, a few receipts from a doctor's office in Boston, a pencil sketch of a street scene he recognized as her hometown, a funeral prayer card for his Uncle Jack's first wife, and ticket stubs from concerts in Newport, Rhode Island during the summer of 1969.

Robert examined it all. He tried to piece it together. "Is this all from before you moved here? You had such adventures, didn't you?"

The old woman blinked. Robert said, "Uncle Jack used to say it was hard to keep up with you." He was trying to be gentle but added. "I never understood what you saw in Matthew Duncan." He rolled his eyes, uncomfortable with her long silences since the stroke. "Maybe that's the point. You always gave us so much love that we couldn't help but reciprocate. Maybe he couldn't help himself either."

She shook her head and labored to rasp, "No. I . . . never deserved . . . love. Forgive me." The old woman drew in a sharp breath that told her perpetual heartbreak. She looked at the locket in his hand and closed her eyes.

II

Matthew Duncan rested his brush atop the palette beside the unfinished canvas and rolled his head to loosen tense joints. He shrugged his shoulders to stretch out his sore back. Each tendon pinged and snapped as he moved. He glanced at the rough sketch he decided to attempt on a canvas larger than he normally used. His eyes flickered back and forth with impatience.

The original sketch had been roughed while the young, fiery-haired woman used an old-fashioned remedy of newspaper to buff the front windows of the bookstore after a neighborhood crew of window washers botched the job. Streaky windows attested to their bungling up and down the shopping district. The town center comprised five tight blocks on her bookstore side and four blocks with the interruption of city hall and the town library on the side he had taken to set up his easel for the day. He had also sketched the window crew who looked to be the scrapings left of daily workers who qualified for little else. They had made a drab composition enlivened only by glimpses of the redhead watching from behind the counter of the bookstore.

He hadn't been interested in her ministrations of the large bay window until her tee-shirt crept out of her waistband and the narrowest slice of white skin first revealed itself between a thick, mannish belt and the bottom edge of her habitual brown, leather bomber. He had seen two men run right into each other on the sidewalk because they were trying to catch her eye. She had been oblivious as usual.

Matt rubbed his chin and examined the unconscious brushwork from his new sable tips. Uncharacteristically, he had focused detail work on two areas out of the normal order of layering a background wash, sketching lines for focus, and then applying the detail work on top. He had spent the early morning on the fine splay of skin between the aged jacket and the mannish belt. The brown leather bomber gave her a jaunty look instead of the usual black that might have rendered her a caricature. The skin exposed by the stretch to wash the top edge of the windowpanes was a pale white velvet, soft like rose petals with a bit of their downy silk. On closer inspection, the bones of her vertebrate knobbed and the beginning swell of rounder flesh below the waist bled to palest pink. He had painted skin that begged to be touched.

The second profusion of color on the canvas was the tumble of glorious red-gold hair she had tossed out of her way with a twist of butcher's cord tied low on her nape. He had spent no fewer than thirty minutes on the brown, twisted string looped into a lopsided bow. The autumn colors of her hair leapt into the brush at about nine this morning and arranged themselves on the canvas. He could have mixed the colors of her glorious hair with his eyes shut. Her hair felt like silk ribbons under his fingers, yet he had never touched her or come more than three feet from her.

He had not been aware of her for the first three months he sketched in the little, riverfront town just thirty minutes south of his studio. When she appeared in a painting that won him some praise, one of the judges mentioned the girl as the focal point. He studied her movements for the next three months and wasted an entire summer wondering exactly how soft her skin might be or the exact texture of her unbound hair. He was satisfied to elude a personal connection with this muse because he told himself she was nondescript and replaceable.

Matthew had decided that she was provincial just like the town. She was a simple girl who favored worn jeans, flowered peasant blouses, grey or black sweaters. When the air grew cool, that worn, oversized leather bomber and tall, weathered boots became her uniform. She worked in a tiny, ancient town in a small bookstore and spent her days encased in mundane tasks highlighted by slavish reading and note-taking. She was probably a student; he assumed history or literature considering the constant study of thick volumes when no one wandered inside the store. She made excellent soup, tolerable sandwiches, and strong coffee for the little bistro carved out of the rows of books and magazines. She smiled for her customers, laughed with an assortment of regulars, and never drove to work. He had concluded that she must live in one of the houses tightly packed into a cross-section of streets that ran from the main road through town and stopped at the waterfront. The rocky banks of the Narragansett limited the sprawl of the small town on that side of the main road which led him home to Newport.

"You've got it bad, Duncan." The nasal, bored voice of the model lounging on the platform behind him startled Matthew out of his study of the emerging figure on the canvas. He had come very close to speaking to the redhead last week when she gave him a crock of soup then glided back to the kitchen without a word. For the first time, he regretted the thickened layer of silence that cloaked him most of the time he studied landscapes. As the voice of his studio-mate's model broke him away from concentration, Matthew realized that the woman in the painting was a landscape. She had escaped the animism of portraiture.

Matthew glanced at the model with deep brown hair pulled to one side as she sat draped in a sheet tossed about her curvy bottom. Roger Markham grumbled behind his sketch pad, "Close your mouth, Bridget. Look out the window, please." Matthew frowned at the bare breasts, the pouty bottom lip and warm, amber eyes of the long-legged woman resting against a couch that had dominated the main platform of the studio for the last three weeks. Part of the urge to continue sketching in Barrington had been avoidance of the salt-scoured voice of this critic. She looked out the window high above them that opened in slices along the ceiling in narrow eyebrow-like openings. She pouted and Roger growled out, "Just say it and then shut your mouth." His voice was gruff and told his impatience with the sketch, his model, and his studio-mate.

Bridget had been flirting with Duncan for months though the big, taciturn man ignored her after their initial flash of intimacy. Roger frowned and drew Matthew into his sketch as he glowered at Bridget. Matthew's sleeves were rolled up to the elbows in folds the exact width of his cuffs. The shirt still looked ironed though he had obviously been preparing the canvas, sketching in the larger figure over a vague background and painting for the last few hours. There was one dab of paint on his dark trousers that looked like the color he had used in another painting to add the redhead into a crowd scene. Roger captured the dazed look on Matthew's face, as Bridget turned her head and growled at the big man, "You're obsessed. I've seen artists get this way, but it doesn't usually last. This has gone on for nearly a year. What's her name?"

Roger closed his eyes and imagined Matthew stepping onto the platform and throttling the woman with his bare hands. No one said such things to Matthew Duncan. The man was glacier cold, unfriendly, and abrasive even toward his friends. A woman he had attracted, discarded, and ignored without even a few pencil or charcoal sketches was below his notice.

Roger tilted his head to consider Bridget in the "woman scorned" role and smiled slightly. If she lived through the afternoon, he would dress her differently for the next composition. She was very beautiful, genuinely warm, and explosively free with her body. He put down his pencil and closed the plastic cover for the palate he had prepared for this canvas. The light had dimmed for the day into afternoon harshness.

Matthew blinked back to them. He had imagined all the overheard conversations in the bookstore and wondered over her name. He looked at her hair and the soft skin of her midriff and remembered that he had avoided visiting her bookstore, her street, even driving through her little town for an entire week.

Who had first mentioned her appearance in his work and made him ultrasensitive a few weeks ago? Who had started his active rejection of her? His agent? His mother?

Matthew's mother had wondered over the name of the town and had frowned over the sensitive faces of the older people. She had wanted to know who the pretty girl might be who posed on her belly in the grass before the old library and read a book. His mother had pushed her lips together and made up a story about the girl that made her sound like a damsel trapped in the vise grip of a mystery. Even Roger had teased that Matthew was keeping his new muse a secret like a mistress in another town.

Matthew glared at the silly, vacant face of classic beauty perched on the couch and hissed, "Her name? Why might I need to know her name? Get out." His voice was colder than he intended. He glanced at Roger expecting some resistance, but his oldest friend nodded and gestured dismissal to Bridget. The other man crossed to the desk to write her a check for the sitting, but Matthew was there before him with twice her usual sitting fee in cash. He placed it directly into her outstretched, quivering hand. His voice was harsh, "It has nothing to do with you who she is. Leave."

Bridget rolled her eyes and arched a perfect brow, "It isn't like I'm going to scratch her eyes out. You obviously had your fill of me that one time. I just hope she realizes what a cold bastard you are before you break her heart. Girls like her are fragile, you know." She shrugged on her blouse as she talked. She tossed a wool skirt over her head and turned to Markham who zipped it for her and kissed her cheek absently.

Pulling on her jacket, Bridget stuffed the money into her pocket and stalked boldly over to the twenty paintings Matthew had finished for a show he and Markham were assembling. She flicked her finger toward one frame after another, "I didn't get it at first. When you sit for extended periods of time, you focus on a far point and let your mind wander. The repetition started bothering me. I noticed this," she glanced back to check for his angry attention. "Not her pretty red hair like you might think—but that would be too obvious like putting a poppy in every painting." Roger grinned at Bridget and grate- fully remembered why he had used her as a model to start; the woman had an agile, sharp mind. "I kept seeing movement—at first, it looked like a dash of a black line that didn't belong—a mistake. Once I noticed it, the movement was in every blasted picture. I couldn't see anything else because of the glare from the overhead lights at that angle."

Matthew was squinting into the canvases from across the room. Now that she pointed it out, from the angle of the plat- form, the pattern was bold. He began to blush, worried that something mundane had unconsciously leaked out of him. Though he pursued painting, the quiet voice of doubt surfaced every few months when his parents hinted about his future or when he noticed the law degree hanging dusty in the apart- ment. He looked closer at the paintings as Bridget toured them.

Her critical essay on the heart of his paintings had con- tinued though he hadn't heard most of it from the boiling blood rushing through his head. Her voice was suddenly harsh enough to pierce his distraction, "Then one afternoon after Roger passed out," she winked at his studio-mate who main- tained silence and a deep frown, "I took a closer look at each place I had noticed the movement, and who did I find?" she grinned and gestured to the large canvas, "Your little, redhead- ed hippie who must be a royal bundle of energy—that girl is always on the move. Look! Even in that commissioned piece for the town library!" She stood before it and pointed to the relaxed figure on the lawn with her book.

Roger finally sputtered, "She's reading; that's hardly pranc- ing across the street." He joined them to examine the paintings.

He knew that Matthew had never intended a motif. Matthew was not an emotional artist who clung to theory but tended to paint what he saw.

Bridget shook her head, "Find the bold black for the movement—she's crossing and re-crossing her ankles. And she's not reading—she's writing something with such concentration, I bet she doesn't notice anything going on around her. Did you think she was reading, Matthew?"

Her amber eyes grew rounder as he stammered instead of answering, "What?" His eyes touched each place the woman with red hair splashed into the scene, teased in his periphery, or grabbed center stage. His heart pounded over her mundane appearance. Other than the hair and the white skin, she was no beauty like Bridget. At first, he thought she was absent in two of the series until he noticed the flutter in a corner or a crowd and found the dark brown jacket or the flash of her long legs. He expelled a breath and looked for other unconscious moments in the paintings. When had he chosen her as his muse? When had her form become the motif for this collection? Was the girl responsible or had it all been happenstance?

Bridget looked at both men and smiled sadly. She felt vindicated in her cruelty toward Matthew Duncan. Just a little affection for the big man let her warn him before she left the studio, "Keep in mind that someone that vibrant and distracted must be just as cold and heartless as you, Matthew Duncan."

She crossed to Roger and kissed him fondly, "Call me if you want me to sit again, Roger."

Matthew withdrew into a grouchier silence than the one that had sent him to the canvases that week. He finished the large painting with the woman stretching to wash the windows at the bookstore buffeted by a frigid New England breeze. Leaves skittered down the sidewalk in the scene and gathered in little piles against the front of the next shop. He waited until the paint was dry before he framed it and took a few pictures for the catalogue slides. He and Roger did not discuss the girl, the painting, or Bridget's disappearance from the studio.

Roger had started a new series of watercolors that he did not show Matthew. Juxtaposed with Matthew's bold oils at a later show, Roger had depicted Matthew Duncan in the throes of creation before introducing himself to the cold, fragile girl from the little town. He had splashed her onto too many pieces to ignore. Years later, Matthew would glance through an exhibition by his friend Roger Markham and wonder what had happened to that solitary, lonely man in the paint strokes.

III

The Griffey's were making a ruckus out of political discussions best left at home over a late breakfast. Catherine rolled her eyes at the young assistant she had just hired for the afternoon shift and continued stamping and shelving the new shipment. If she popped her head around the corner from "Romance" and "Adventure," she might be asked some controversial question that would propel her into the fray. Catherine yanked her hair back into an actual knot and decided to ignore them unless they started breaking plates.

Nana Griffey had entered the shop earlier and accosted Catherine while aged Felix talked the ear off the barber at the corner. Her husband Felix would have stopped the rough question midair, "Catherine, my cherub! Where has that admirer of yours gone? That artist fellow. Have you chased him off, rude girl?" Catherine had let her eyebrows rise. Of course, she had noticed the absence of the man who sketched in the shop nearly every day for months.

Catherine had shaken her head and cleared the table next

to the old lady. "He's no admirer of mine," she had whispered. She had slipped behind the counter to ready the Griffey's tray with the usual fare: two coffees with extra in a carafe, water for requisite pills, two fresh scones, jam, and clotted cream. Catherine's mother supplied the clotted cream for the regulars who expected a casual high tea version of scones. Catherine had introduced the scones when she first returned from Boston a month after her pilot died. All time in her recent past was marked by his death in a helicopter crash into a Vietnamese jungle.

Nana had chortled over Catherine's denial. "You must be blind, girl. The man does nothing but gaze at you and sketch. Mark my words—the man's besotted." Catherine Gibson had laughed and felt a little sorry for the man if he ever returned. The old folks had grown bold in his absence. The stranger who sketched for hours had perfected the dull, removed blankness necessary to stay out of the tumult among the regulars. These people had been arguing in public well before Catherine's birth twenty-four years ago.

The older patrons, old school friends who were now married, her siblings, and sometimes, even her parents acted as though she was missing something without a mate. Catherine had chosen a mate who had been a friend and a lover, and he was gone. She had carried their child like a grudging souvenir since his last deployment and used her grief to slough it away. Her hand unwittingly rested on her flat abdomen and felt for the slight protrusion that had deflated quickly after the visit to the doctor while she was still numb from the telegram. Hindsight purchased a curious lump of relieved regret under her palm.

Catherine unpacked the books in the "History" area of nonfiction and ran her fingers over the spines of wars. In her secret heart, the death of her pilot had been more than a tragedy with one man's life taken and myriad others disturbed. She had felt just a twinge of relief after the first onslaught of sorrow.

Just over the barrier of two rows of books, chairs were being scraped across the floor, and someone was calling out, "Help!" Catherine rushed toward the bistro area and found Felix Griffey being eased to the floor by the large man they had speculated about earlier. Felix was slightly gray in the face.

"Was he eating? Could he be choking?" Catherine hurried over to listen for Nana's answer and loosen Felix's constant knotted tie that looked greased and permanent. The old silk thing unraveled under her fingers, and she thought she heard the intake of a reed-thin breath.

The big man inserted a finger into the old man's mouth and felt for an obstruction. "Nothing," he muttered. He glanced up to Catherine and sucked in a sharper breath, "Turquoise?" He blinked and tried again, "Ambulance?"

She nodded and looked toward the counter as a customer used the phone attached to the bistro wall. Someone else had run down the block to the doctor's office to fetch help in person. Felix's breath wheezed through a constricted airway, but he breathed on his own. Catherine found herself trembling when the doctor and the paramedics rushed into the store at the same time. It was a relief to relinquish control.

As she got shakily to her feet, the artist rose also and peered at her from the distance of a table. His eyes, she thought, were the milky blue of a clear sky. She fixed his age at forty, height about six-two and just as habitually formal in attire as Felix. His silk tie was gentry green with a tiny gray stripe that exactly matched his fine, gray jacket. Perhaps she had noticed him. His hands trembled like hers.

He sighed as they were shoved out of the way by the crowd of responders. His breath was short, and voice hushed, "Turquoise. I got your eyes exactly right." Slumped on a chair watching the professionals revive her Felix, Nana Griffey cackled and clapped her hands in vindication.

IV

Showing the locket to her brother in the haze of a few too many beers, Catherine tapped his knuckles because he had let his jaw drop comically slack as he looked at the intimate pair in the miniature and then narrowed his eyes at her face. He suddenly looked more like a father and less like the older brother she had chosen from six other siblings to become her friend. Men did not usually write their sisters long, descriptive narratives, but her brother Jack used his once silent baby sister as confessor. Catherine warned him not to turn into all gruff, protective urges with that sharp tap again at the joint where his thumb joined his hand. He winced and drew in a breath. "The painter is in love with you then?"

Catherine winced in return and shook her head, "He seeks possession." She took another sip then said, "I don't think he understands love." She glanced at the tiny painting cradled in her brother's large palm. He held it like a little creature, like he had cupped the head of his youngest daughter during the baptism Catherine attended during the first hazy month of grief after her pilot's death.

She thought of Jack and Tessa gazing at the child's face, beatified by the streaming colors of the octagonal stained glass pouring light into the vestibule where the priest stood before them. That was love. Looking up to answer the old man's call to repeat the vows said for the child, Catherine remembered meeting the priest's glazed eyes. That had been the moment she knew Tessa wasn't merely wan and sick with post-birth exhaustion. Jack had said there had been tests, there was a tumor; they were talking operations and treatments. Tessa wasn't going to live much longer, said the tears in the eyes of their old priest. He intoned the baptismal prayers by rote, anointed the tiny head and finally woke the baby with the trickle of water over her forehead and into her dark gold hair. Catherine remembered glancing up to her brother, the only one she called her friend among a pack of siblings and praying she could begin to feel enough to help him.

Years gathered in the corner of the pub where they sat barraged by loud conversations around the bar and rock music blaring from the band. In the smoky bar, Jack looked at his little sister who was wearing the same grey sweater in the painting. In the miniature, her hair corkscrewed streaky red and gold in low light and added contrast against the man's white shirt. His face was partially obscured because he leaned in to kiss her neck. The man abjectly adored her with his hands splayed at her hip and belly as if he treasured her.

Jack looked up to examine his sister's beautiful turquoise eyes. The artist had captured their color exactly; he had also given her eyes the gem-like cold that betrayed a long time of study. Jack closed the locket and ran one finger over the fine carnelian stone affixed to the lid. It felt warm like blood. "He understands love, my darling sister. I don't know that you understand it. I don't know that you're capable of it, Catherine." Jack grimaced over the truth and understood her frown as he gave the locket back to her.

She didn't deny his words or sulk over his bluntness. She held the locket in her tight fist for a few minutes before slipping it into the pocket of her pilot's jacket.

Rock, River, Child

I stare out at the river, rock the baby, and think about killing Andrew. I never thought I'd ever get away from him. Twelve Tree Island should have been idyllic—a few acres of rock, scrubby grass, and trees—white pines, scrub oaks, one weeping willow, several wild cherries, and one red maple framing a cedar-shingled house on the Saint Lawrence River. Rather charming except for Andrew.

You know how disasters come in threes? Last fall semester went like this: I slept with the wrong guy, became pregnant, and then agreed to meet my assistant's rich uncle. I had been warned—Uncle Andrew had "quirks" but he was "loaded" and owned his own island up north. He did like wearing the same clothes over and over until they shredded. True—his hair was overlong, but it curled in dark blond spirals, mercifully hiding his fraying shirt collar. His icy blue eyes were surrounded by laugh lines; he thought he was funny—always. When we met, his opening line was harsh. "So, you're the knocked-up professor," he said and toasted me, grinning as he sloshed whiskey onto his shirt.

I think I backed up a step.

"It's okay. I like babies," he said as he toasted my middle with another splash.

I mumbled, "Excuse me," and left him to his drink. When my assistant asked how our conversation went, I rolled my eyes.

Andrew started turning up: he sat in on my poetry reading, he showed up after an evening class and walked me to my car, and he apologized for our awkward, first meeting. He appeared in my regular coffee shop. We did not date but talked and drank pots of tea. Andrew was well-read and comfortably shabby. The baby's father wasn't answering my texts, but Andrew hovered.

As I rounded my sixth month, he invited me out to his island. "You'll love it." His eyes glittered coldly as they rested on the baby. "Pack for the weekend—my niece is coming, too." The weekend was restful, but I woke groggy on Monday, and found I was marooned—my assistant gone with the boat. His eyes were so cold as he spooned eggs onto plates at the table. "I want to go home now."

I remember shrinking into a ball as Andrew threw plates, mugs, books—anything, then punched at walls until the fit left him. Of course, Andrew begged for forgiveness, and I kept quiet and watched. The silence became unnerving with the river casting reflections on the plain walls, and both of us watching.

Before I crept upstairs to bed, he asked me, "Why do you ever need to go back?" Each morning, I asked to leave. Andrew grew tense but stopped smashing things. Sometimes he crooned, "Don't worry, Meredith. I'll take care of the baby."

Every day I walked the shoreline. Ice crusted the river rocks as winter advanced. Sometimes I stared at a distant bridge visible through bare branches. Despite Andrew's warning to stay on the walks, I slipped into woods on the northern end looking for a place to hide. Andrew's anger left me shaken, and recently, a window had been shattered.

Stumbling over a root one morning, I noticed a figure sitting under an oak. Reaching her, I could not stifle my scream— the deflated face of a decaying woman peeked out from burlap barely covering her body. Heart pounding, I searched for other trees surrounded by burlap. There was a person under each one—shielded barely by leaves and decaying cloth. Twelve open graves—twelve special trees.

I slammed back into the house. This time I was crazy—throwing everything I could at him—words, books, crockery.

"Calm down," he whispered, "I didn't kill them. I offered each of them a place to stay. To stay and have their babies."

Andrew confessed it all—wanting a child, meeting young women who trusted too easily, each birth, and each death. "I hope you survive the birth, Meredith," he mumbled, "but I'm not a very good midwife."

Another month raced by like the current. Another walk like all the others but this one at frozen dawn. This time a splash of color against the rocks alerted me to a wooden rowboat caught by tree roots. I clambered over the riprap, maneuvered it to a pushing off point, and stepped into its sturdy bottom. One lone oar rested at my feet.

Above me on the path, Andrew ran, almost tumbling. Over the rushing water, he screamed—"Meredith! No!"

I dipped the oar. Shoving off deep, I felt the boat jerk and then slip out into the rough water. I looked back.

Andrew raced ahead on land. He screamed—his face masked in anger.

I drew the oar back and dipped wildly.

He roared over the river. "Stay with me, Merry." Then he launched himself into the river.

The boat rocked every time I used the oar to push off rocks stationed to catch me. One wild swing of the oar, and Andrew clutched onto the gunnel.

I struck his head. I hit him again—his hands, his face, but he did not let go. He spat water, maybe blood, and erupted, "You crazy cow, I'll never let you go!"

We broke free of the island and were caught by the current rushing past other islands toward the great green bridge. Andrew tried to hoist himself up.

Mesmerized with horror, I froze for a second. I stood, breath heaving as I clutched at the oar. He lurched upward—one arm and half his chest—almost toppling me out of the boat. Stepping back, I shoved the oar with all the weight of my body into the crevice between his head and his chest. He grasped at the oar and grinned.

I pushed into his hand and forced him underwater. The river washed his long hair over his face, one of his hands still clutched the side of the boat. I kicked at him, overbalanced, and doubled over toward him. I looked down—right into his eyes. "You are fucking insane," I thought, staring into those watery ice-blue eyes.

I held the oar tight and watched the water rush over his face and snatch at his hair, clothes trailing.

The boat's bottom slammed into rocks, and he let go. His mouth open, his body tumbling, the river took him away.

I take the baby everywhere—the university, the grocery store, and the island. A body was found stuck in a cradle of logs after the thaw. This morning, I reported Andrew missing.